The Last Stubborn Buffalo in Nevada

Stephen Bly

CROSSWAY BOOKS • WHEATON, ILLINOIS
A DIVISION OF GOOD NEWS PUBLISHERS

The Last Stubborn Buffalo in Nevada.

Copyright © 1993 by Stephen Bly.

Published by Crossway Books
    A division of Good News Publishers
    1300 Crescent St.
    Wheaton, Illinois 60187.

Cover illustration: David Yorke

First printing, 1993

Printed in the United States of America

For a list of other books by Stephen Bly or information regarding speaking engagements, write: Stephen Bly, Winchester, ID 83555.

Library of Congress Cataloging-in-Publication Data
Bly, Stephen A. 1944-
    The last stubborn buffalo in Neveda / Stephen Bly.
        p.   cm.—(Nathan T. Riggins western adventure series: bk.#4)   CJF
    Summary: Nathan soon realizes the buffalo he has recently aquired   Bly
belongs in a zoo; and after praying for financial means to move his
animal there, a dramatic solution presents itself.
    [1. Bison—Fiction. 2. Frontier and pioneer life—Neveda—Fiction
3. Neveda—Fiction.] I. Title. II. Series: Bly, Stephen A., 1944-
Nathan T. Riggins western adventure series; bk. 4.
PZ7.B6275Las 1993   [Fic]—dc20   93-8654
ISBN 0-89107-746-4   126p,

01   00   99   98   97   96   95   94
15   14   13   12   11   10   9   8   7   6   5   4   3   2

*For
Hoss*

1

Nathan T. Riggins felt foolish dressed in his Sunday clothes on a Friday afternoon.

"Hey, Nathan! What are you doing?"

"I'm waiting for a stage. What does it look like?"

Colin Maddison, Jr., (with two *d*'s) carried his canvas coat in his hand as he sat down on the rough wooden bench in front of the Nevada Central Stage Line office.

"Where're you going? Where are your parents? They're not letting you go off on the stage by yourself, are they?" he quizzed.

"I'm not going anywhere," Nathan mumbled.

"You're waiting for someone, right? Is it your mom? Your grandparents? Listen, if someone famous is coming in on the stage, I ought to know about it," Colin insisted. "I mean . . . my dad's the president of the bank, and surely he—"

"I don't want to talk about it." Nathan sulked, rubbing his fingers through his light brown hair and replacing his hat on his head.

"You're waiting for someone you don't want to wait for?" Colin pressed. "Did your mother make you come wait for some old aunt or second cousin? That's okay. I'll wait with you."

"You don't have to stay. And I'm not waiting for a relative. And, no, my mother didn't make me do anything."

7

"Well . . . if your mother didn't make you, why are you here?"

"I was wondering the same thing." Nathan sighed. He stared north down Main Street and glanced at the green mountains in the distance.

"Hey, you want to go hunt some rabbits?" Colin asked. "Maybe you'd let me ride Onepenny."

"I can't go hunting, Colin. I promised Leah I'd wait at the stage."

"Leah! Leah made you do this? Come on, Riggins. You aren't going to let some girl with freckles run your life, are you?"

Nathan tugged at his collar trying to release his tie. Then he sprang up, ambled across the wooden plank sidewalk, and gazed at a mule-pulled freight wagon creaking towards the Galena Mercantile.

"I'm not letting Leah run my life. I just made her a promise, that's all. And I've got to keep my word."

"So Leah's expecting company, and you're the one to meet the stage?"

"Yep."

"Well, who is it?"

"Who is what?"

"Who is the person you're waiting for?" Colin shouted waving his hands in the air.

"Some friend of Leah's."

"Ah hah!" Colin jabbered. "Now I get it. Some cute girlfriend of Leah's is coming to town, and you slicked up to make a good impression."

"Hardly."

"What's she look like? Is she our age? Did you get to see a picture of her?"

"He. It's a he."

"You're waiting for a boy?" Colin gasped.

"Yeah, and it's about the dumbest thing I ever did." He jammed his hands into his pockets.

"Why did you agree to it?"

"'Cause Leah was crying, that's why," Nathan reported.

"Well, anyway . . ." Colin banged his boot heels as he sauntered closer to Nathan. "What's this guy's name?"

"Kylie Collins," Nathan mumbled.

"What! Here in Galena? The infamous Kylie Collins?"

"Yeah, the guy Leah 'ain't ever goin' to marry nobody else but.' Mr. Kylie Collins himself."

"Why in the world isn't Leah here?" Colin asked.

"It 'ain't proper to look over-anxious,'" Nathan quoted.

"Leah said that?"

"Yep."

"This is stupid," Colin chided.

"I already said that," Nathan reminded him. "How about you going for a walk or something? Don't make a big deal out of it."

"You've got to be kidding! I wouldn't miss this for anything on earth. I can see the story in *Frank Leslie's Illustrated Weekly* already. 'Fight to the finish in the streets of Galena, Nevada, as two lads battle to the death for the hand of the lovely Miss Leah Walker!'" Colin giggled.

Nathan scowled. "I think your mother is calling you for supper." He motioned toward the bank.

"Forget it, Riggins. I'm staying right here. You can't sucker me."

"Well then, there's no use telling you about the factory-made creme fills shipped all the way from St. Louis that just came into the Mercantile," Nathan added.

"Creme fills?"

"Mine were raspberry . . . but they have lemon, orange, strawberry, and cherry."

"Riggins, if you're lying . . ."

Nathan turned back to the bench and sat down. "Do I ever lie?"

"Dark chocolate or milk chocolate?"

"Both."

"How much do they cost?"

"Two for a nickel."

Colin stared down Main Street toward the north. "I don't see the stage."

"Me either."

"I think maybe I should go check out those creme fills." Colin grabbed his coat and hurried down the sidewalk.

Nathan leaned back on the bench, jerked his tie loose, and unbuttoned the top button on his white shirt. He crammed the black silk tie into his shirt pocket and then walked into the stage office.

"Mr. Olivera, how late is the stage now?"

The short man in the green trousers and tall boots pulled out his pocket watch.

"It's a good hour late, Nathan. Must have got stuck crossing the river again. It's been a bad week for that. All this spring runoff slows the route down."

"Stuck? How long will it take to get it unstuck?"

"Tuesday last they didn't roll into town until 5:25."

"5:25! I can't wait that long. Maybe I'll ride out to the river and see if I can lend a hand."

"I wouldn't go in those clothes," Mr. Olivera cautioned. "There's lots of mud at the river."

Within fifteen minutes Nathan had run home, changed clothes, left a note for his mom, and saddled Onepenny. He had just led his spotted horse out of the Lander County Livery and parked him next to the corrals when a scream caused him to spin back toward town.

"Nathan T. Riggins, you promised me that you'd wait for the stage!" Leah cried. She held up her long dress and ran down the dusty street.

"I did wait!" he hollered.

"But you ain't waitin' now! And where's them nice clothes you promised?"

"Leah, you saw me! I waited right there for over an hour. The stage is late. Mr. Olivera said it might be stuck in the river again, so I'm ridin' out to see if I can help them get it going again."

"Why ain't you wearin' your good clothes? You don't want Kylie to see you lookin' like that, do ya?"

"I don't care if Kylie ever sees me at all." Nathan mounted Onepenny and turned him north. "It's you he's coming to visit, isn't it?"

"It certainly is . . . and I'm going with you."

"You are not."

"Am too!" she insisted.

"You can't go . . . it isn't proper for a girl to look too anxious."

"Who said that?"

"You did."

"Well . . . I lied. Come on, Nathan, please? You know I been waitin' a year for Kylie to come visit . . . please, let me ride with you!"

"Leah, you are the most aggravating girl I've ever met!" Nathan reached down, grabbed Leah's arm, and pulled her up behind him on the horse. She fussed at keeping her dress pulled down while sitting side-saddle behind the cantle.

"Well, that's jist because you ain't met many girls!" she finally replied.

■

About a half-mile out of town, Nathan's gray and white dog, Tona, trotted out of the sagebrush and took up the lead, just a few steps ahead of Onepenny.

Leah laced the loose leather strings behind the cantle of Nathan's saddle around her wrists and shook her hair loose as she bounced along in the mild spring breeze that blew from the northwest.

"Nathan, ain't them hills pretty?"

"Yep."

"You are really going to like Kylie—honest," she insisted.

"That's what you keep saying."

"Now you ain't jealous, are you? I mean, I always told you that I ain't never going to marry nobody but Kylie Collins."

"I'm not jealous, Leah. I know you're in love with this Kylie boy."

"I didn't say I loved him," she corrected.

"But you're going to marry him someday!" Nathan pointed out.

"Yeah, but I never did say that I loved him, so don't you go puttin' no words in my mouth!"

"But how could you—"

"The trouble with you, Nathan T. Riggins, is that you jist don't understand women."

Lord, I don't know about women . . . but I know I don't understand this girl!

The snows of winter and the heavy rain in early April had decorated the mountains north of Galena with dark green grass. It was bunched here and there between the sage, but from a distance the landscape all looked solid green to Nathan. It was his first spring in Nevada, and he marveled that the barren hills could look so lush. Even the tailing piles scattered by the diggings of frustrated miners sprouted grass among the rusts and yellows of discarded gravel.

"You know, Leah, when all the mines are played out, this sure would make good country for a cattle ranch."

"Are you going to be a rancher when you grow up . . . or a lawman like your daddy? I sure hope you won't be a lawman."

"Why?"

"'Cause you'd bring your wife nothin' but aggravation and worry—always wondering if you would get shot or somethin'. Jist like when your Daddy got shot last winter."

"He's all right now," Nathan reminded her.

"Sure, but it was mighty close."

"Well, I'll probably be a rancher . . . or maybe governor," he teased.

"Governor? Boy, that'll be the day. Governor Nathan T. Riggins." Leah paused for a moment and then said softly, "I'd vote for ya."

"Women can't vote."

"Well . . . it won't make no difference. You wouldn't win. My daddy says all them politicians is crooked, and you don't ever cheat, lie, or nothin' like that."

For about an hour they bounced along with only brief conversations. Finally, Leah waved her hand at a dark ribbon of foliage stretching out ahead of them.

"Look!" She pointed at the trees. "There's the crossing!"

Two rapping sounds caused Nathan to pull Onepenny up.

"Someone's shooting!" he cautioned.

"It's a holdup! They're shootin' at the robbers. We better hurry and help them."

"I don't think it's a holdup," Nathan commented. "Look,

they're pulling the wagon out of the mud . . . and over there those men are target-practicing or something."

"Maybe Kylie's shootin'. Did I ever tell you what a good shot he is?"

"No, but I did figure out he is perfect in every way," Nathan mumbled.

"Are you sure you ain't jist a little bit jealous?" Leah asked.

Nathan didn't bother answering. He rode straight toward the stagecoach.

"Hi, Mr. Davis . . . did the stage get stuck again?"

"Nate . . . you ride out from town? Miss Walker . . . are you two out for a little picnic?" He raised his eyebrows.

"We ain't on no picnic," Leah replied.

"We were worried about you being so late," Nathan informed him.

"Well, I sure appreciate the concern. I just pulled her out. Now as soon as I scrape the mud off and get the passengers reloaded, we'll be back on the road."

"Is that the passengers up on the knoll?"

"Yep, three fellas. Two are headed to Austin, and the other's gettin' off in Galena."

"It must be Kylie!" Leah exclaimed.

"I don't reckon I heard a name," Mr. Davis reported. "Say, will you two ride up there and tell them to come on back now. They ain't going to bring down that old boy at that distance with handguns anyway."

"What are they shooting at?"

"Oh, that bull buffalo that's been wandering around out here all winter."

"Buffalo! Thunder? They can't do that!" Nathan hollered. "That buffalo belongs to the Rocky Mountain Exposition Company!"

"Well, it's been a nuisance all winter. It rammed this stage last week! It's crazy!"

"I got to stop them!" Nathan spurred Onepenny, and the spotted horse burst into a gallop with Nathan's dog, Tona, barking ahead of them. Nathan took a hard left turn when he hit the mud at the edge of the river. He heard a scream and felt Leah losing her grip around his waist. She tumbled off the back of the horse, but Nathan didn't look back.

Lord, don't let them shoot Thunder! It wasn't his idea to get stranded out here!

Nathan could see two men and a boy standing on a hill with smoking revolvers in their hands.

"Hey! Stop! You can't do that! Don't shoot him!" he screamed. Tona sprinted at the men barking incessantly.

The three looked surprised as they turned to stare at Nathan galloping up the hill. Nathan figured the boy in the middle to be a couple of years older than himself.

That's Kylie Collins? He's not much bigger than me . . . and he's not all that strong.

"I say," one of the men called to Nathan, "what's all the screaming about? You startled that bison. How will we shoot it now?"

Nathan stood in his stirrups and looked out across the prairie at Thunder, who stood about a hundred yards away, facing them, but no longer retreating.

"You can't shoot that buffalo . . . it belongs to the Rocky Mountain Exposition Company of North Platte, Nebraska."

"You're lyin'," the blond-haired boy answered. "You can't own a buffalo!"

One of the men raised his pistol to fire another shot.

"No . . . wait!" Nathan insisted. "I'm telling the truth. You see, Dakota Williams and his Rocky Mountain Show were on the train going to San Francisco last fall, and Thunder

—that's the buffalo's name—busted out of the cattle car and ran off. They couldn't catch him, so they had to go on. But last winter I found him, and I've been bringing him a little feed now and then. I wrote to Mr. Williams, and he said that they would pick up Thunder on their way back to North Platte in the spring."

"That's absurd," the man said and again lifted his gun.

Nathan spurred Onepenny in front of the man blocking his view.

"I say . . . move that horse!" the man commanded.

"Look," Nathan reasoned, "Mr. Davis said it's time to load the stage."

"Not without downing that bison," the man insisted.

"You can't kill it with a handgun from here. You'll just wound it and make it mad. Then it will charge you, and someone will get hurt."

"Well, that would be one way to get it close enough to shoot," the boy chimed in.

"Nobody's going to shoot that buffalo!"

The boy took two steps to the left of Onepenny and raised his gun. Nathan dove out of the saddle and knocked the boy to the ground. The revolver tumbled into the sage. Tona pounced into the fight barking and biting at the other boy's heels.

Both boys struggled to their feet. Nathan ducked, but the fist still caught him in the side of his neck just below his left ear. The blow made him stagger back.

Oh, man . . . he's bigger than me!

Diving below the next wild swing, Nathan tackled the boy to the ground and threw a punch to the midsection. He felt his knuckles sink into the soft flesh below the rib cage. Suddenly, a knee slammed into Nathan's stomach, and he rolled over trying to catch his breath.

The other boy was on his feet, and Nathan recovered in time to grab a shoe as the boy kicked at his side. He twisted the foot sharply to the right, and the boy let out a piercing scream just about the time Nathan heard two guns fire.

"You busted my ankle!" the boy cried. "You broke it!"

The boy stumbled back and fell to the ground clutching his ankle.

"My word!" one of the men shouted. "That beast is actually going to charge us!"

Tona was still barking as Nathan looked up to see Thunder begin his charge from across the prairie. The two men ran for the river.

"Wait! Uncle Jed! Help me!" the boy yelled as the buffalo pounded toward them.

Nathan leaped into the saddle and stationed Onepenny between the buffalo and the boy on the ground. The spotted horse spun his hindquarters toward the charging animal.

"Stay, Onepenny . . . stay!"

Tona barked.

Onepenny nervously pranced.

Thunder shook the prairie.

The boy on the ground cried.

Nathan prayed.

The buffalo ran straight at Nathan and then, only twenty yards in front of them, suddenly swerved off to the left and pursued the men running toward the river. He didn't slow until both men dove headfirst into the swollen stream.

Then Thunder pulled up, peered at the men, turned, and slowly walked back out into the prairie, never glancing back at the confusion behind him.

Nathan jumped down and patted his horse's neck. "That-a-boy, Onepenny . . . good horse! You stayed with me again, didn't you."

Tona slinked off into the sage eyeing the buffalo.

"I can't believe it!" the boy on the ground marveled. "You and that horse blocked off that stampeding buffalo!"

"Onepenny's a good horse. We've had run-ins with that old boy before."

"Look," said the boy wiping the tears from his cheeks, "I'm sorry about the fight. I was . . . you know . . . mad."

"Well, just don't go shootin' animals for the fun of it. He really does belong to Dakota Williams."

"Can you help me back to the stage? My ankle is busted."

Nathan slipped the reins over the saddle horn, and Onepenny trailed along behind them. Nathan let the boy hold on to his shoulder as he limped back to the stage.

It wasn't until they got to the stage that he remembered Leah. She was hunkered down on a log trying to wipe the mud off her face.

"You ruined my good dress, Nathan T. Riggins!" she cried. "Look at this! Look at this! How could you do this to me?"

"Leah, I'm sorry . . . it's just that they were shooting at . . . Thunder." He noticed that the boy was staring at Leah.

"Oh, yeah . . . listen. Eh . . . this really is Leah Walker, and her dress was very pretty, and before I dumped her into the mud, she looked great!" Nathan stammered. "'Course there's no need for me to introduce you two. I'm really sorry, Leah. I know this isn't the way you wanted it to go."

"What are you talking about?" She sniffled.

"I know you wanted to look pretty for Kylie and—"

"That ain't Kylie!" she whispered

"It isn't?" Then he turned to the boy. "Who are you?"

"Eh . . . Mason DeLaney. Who's she?"

"Leah Walker, a friend . . . a good friend of mine."

"Well, I ain't your friend no more! You treat me bad, Nathan T. Riggins. You really treat me bad!"

■

Mr. Davis finally got his passengers loaded up. Leah, partially clean, rode behind Nathan as they began to trot back to town.

"Say, you two!" Davis shouted. "I jist 'membered. I got a letter for each of you in the dispatch."

"A letter?" Leah smiled.

"Yep. Here they are." He swung down off the stage and handed them up to Nathan. "Ain't no reason for you to wait until I get to town."

2

Onepenny trotted beside a wagon rut toward Galena as Nathan and Leah bounced and ripped their letters open.

"He ain't comin'!" she moaned. "They're goin' straight to Silver City from Fort Hall, and they ain't comin' down here!"

"I don't believe it!" Nathan shouted.

"You'd better believe it. It says so right here."

"Man, this must be my lucky day! It's an answer to prayer!" Nathan laughed.

Leah reached up and wiped a tear from her cheek. "Nathan, you ain't got no right to be funnin' me about this!"

"Wait until I tell everybody in town!" Nathan shouted waving his letter back at Leah.

Suddenly, Leah wound up and slugged Nathan in the right arm, causing him to clutch the saddle horn to keep from sliding off the horse.

"What did you do that for?" he hollered, rubbing the ripe bruise.

"'Cause you're making sport of me and . . ." Now the tears were streaming down her face. "And cause I'm all covered with mud, and Kylie ain't comin', and cause I cain't learn my lines to the play, and—"

"Kylie's not coming to see you?" Nathan asked.

"Of course he ain't! I read you the letter."

"Oh, yeah . . . your letter. Who was it from?"

Leah brushed her long brown hair back from her eyes. "I told you it was from Kylie! Weren't you listenin'?"

"I, eh . . . I guess I got sidetracked with my letter," he admitted.

"Who is your letter from?" Leah spoke softly now.

"It's from Dakota Williams," Nathan reported.

"Honest?"

"Yep. So what happened to Kylie Collins?" Nathan stood in the stirrups and stretched his legs.

"You really weren't makin' fun of me, were you? Nathan, I'm sorry I hit you." Leah reach up and rubbed Nathan's arm where she had clobbered him.

Nathan pulled up Onepenny and stopped. Then he turned and glanced at the tear-streaked freckles across the bridge of her nose. "Have you been crying?"

"Yeah."

"I'm real sorry, Leah. Honest, I am." Nathan tried to comfort her.

"Listen, all I said was that Kylie and his parents are goin' on to the Idaho mines, and they ain't comin' down."

"I know how much you were looking forward to this. Maybe he can come down in the summer."

"Yeah . . . maybe," she murmured.

Nathan spurred Onepenny, and they trotted toward town. Both were quiet for a minute.

"She'll be really mad at me," Leah finally said.

"Who?"

"My stepmother. She told me to save this dress for church. I snuck it out and wore it anyway. She can get mule-cross when she's mad."

"Why don't you stop at my house and let my mother

21

wash it out for you? She's good at getting mud out of my clothes."

"Nathan?"

"Yeah?"

"If you weren't funnin' me, then what were you hollering about?"

"Oh! It's my letter. Listen to this!

Dear Master Nathan T. Riggins,

I received your note concerning my buffalo, Thunder, on April 4. I appreciate your seeing that he had plenty to eat this winter. Unfortunately, the Rocky Mountain Exposition Show was rained out for twenty-one straight days, and I had to disband the company.

Not all is lost. I've been elected Mayor of Stockton and plan to settle here for a while. All of this is to say that I will not be coming back through Nevada to pick up Thunder. So here is my offer. I will sell Thunder to you for the price of $1.00. Just sign both copies of the bill of sale, and mail one copy to me with a dollar, and the buffalo is yours.

If you learn how to keep him in a pen, you're a better man than I am.

Yours truly,
Dakota Williams

"Can you believe it? I'm going to own a buffalo!"

"Why?"

"Why, what?"

Leah grabbed Nathan's waist as Onepenny picked up the

pace. "Why do you want to own a buffalo? You goin' to butcher it?"

"Butcher it? Are you crazy?" Nathan moaned. "Haven't you been reading the newspapers? They're shooting all the buffalo on the eastern slope and plains. Daddy says someday buffalo will be as rare as a cool day in July. And I'll own one. Me, Nathan T. Riggins, buffalo rancher."

"One buffalo don't make a ranch," she protested.

"Leah, you just don't have any vision. Can't you see? I'll be the only kid in Nevada who owns a buffalo."

"You're the only kid in Nevada that wants one."

"Look, you don't understand, do you? I own a buffalo! Not even old Kylie Collins can say that!"

Leah was quiet for a few minutes.

"Nathan?"

"Yeah."

"You was just a little jealous of Kylie, weren't ya?"

Nathan was silent.

"Yeah," he finally admitted. "I was a little jealous."

"Thanks, Nathan," she whispered.

"For what?"

"For sayin' you was jealous. It makes me feel good."

"I wasn't lying."

"I know—you don't ever lie."

Nathan thought for a moment he could feel Leah holding tighter to his waist. Then she turned loose and grabbed the saddle strings.

"Were you serious about your mama washing my dress?" she finally asked.

"Sure. She's good at that kind of thing."

"What do you think she'll say?"

"About the dress?"

23

"No, about the buffalo," Leah said impatiently. "What will your parents say when you tell them you own a buffalo?"

"Oh, I'm sure they'll be impressed by my ingenuity."

■

"You did what?" Nathan's mother roared as she scrubbed Leah's dress across the washboard.

"I bought Thunder, the buffalo, for only a dollar. I already mailed Mr. Williams the money, and I've got the bill of sale—see. It's all legal and—"

"What in the world are you going to do with a buffalo?" she grilled.

"Why does everyone keep asking me that?" Nathan complained. "Nobody ever asks, 'What are you going to do with a dog?' or 'What are you going to do with a horse?'"

"Dogs don't require a corral and four tons of hay! And you can't ride a buffalo! If he stampedes again and runs over a wagon or something, you will now be responsible," his father lectured.

"That's just the point. I'll keep him safe in a corral, and he won't bother anyone, and no one will bother him."

"What corral?"

"Shipley's. The bank owns the place now that the Shipleys moved to Arizona Territory, and Mr. Maddison said I could use the corral until the place is sold."

"That corral won't hold a newborn calf, let alone a 2,500-pound buffalo," Mr. Riggins insisted.

"But me and Colin and Leah can patch it up. Don't you see, Dad? Galena will be the only town in Nevada with its very own buffalo."

"And I'm the marshal in Galena. If that animal causes trouble, I'll shoot it. Have you got that clear?"

"Yes, sir! Does this mean I get to keep him?"

"Until we get hungry enough to butcher it. But I'm not going to help you bring it in. If you can sweet-talk it into Shipley's corral, then you can keep it. I'm not paying for hay, and I'm not haulin' manure. Do you understand?"

"Yes, sir. As soon as summer vacation starts, I can double my hours at the Mercantile. I'll buy plenty of hay this summer."

"You've got to get him rounded up first," his father reminded him.

"David," Mrs. Riggins asked her husband, "do you think Nathan can bring that buffalo in by himself? I mean, would it be safe?"

"I think," Marshal Riggins said as he pulled on his hat, "that if he can't get it to town, it doesn't belong to him." Then right before he left the house, he turned back. "And whatever you do, don't try to rope it."

"Yes, sir . . . I'll remember," Nathan blurted out.

■

By 8:00 A.M. Saturday, Nathan had his crew rounded up. Leah, wearing an old dark dress and a hat pulled down on her head, rode a roan mare. Colin, sporting his woolly chaps and spurs on his boots, rode his father's buckskin gelding.

Nathan tied Onepenny to the Shipley corral gate. Tona had already sniffed the corrals and was turning circles in preparation for a nap in the shade.

"We got to build fence first," Nathan reminded them.

"It looks all right to me," Colin offered.

"It wouldn't curb a calf," Nathan responded. "Your dad said we could use those rails in the barn." Nathan waved his hand at a stack of long boards.

"He did?"

"Yep. Come on. You guys hold a rail up, and I'll nail it tight."

While Leah held one end of the board, Colin hoisted the other. With both hands clutching the hammer handle, Nathan pounded twenty-penny common nails to attach the rail to the posts.

"There are forty-one loose boards in this corral and eleven that are missing completely. Did you know that you'll have to drive in seventy-three nails? If each one takes about ten blows, Nathan . . . you'll have to pound nails 730 times to finish the job," Colin called out.

"Yeah . . . thanks, Colin," Nathan moaned. "That should keep me busy for a while."

"How does he figure all of that out?" Leah asked.

"Why does he figure all of that out?" Nathan countered.

"Hey," Colin yelled, "it's boring holding boards. When are we going to go cowboying?"

"When we have a buffalo-tight fence," Nathan called back.

"You think this will hold him?" Leah asked.

"A five-rail fence of rough-cut two-by-eights nailed onto railroad ties sunk four feet into the ground—yeah, it will hold him. Thunder's kind of peaceful as long as you don't get him riled."

"Colin's right. It is boring just standing here."

"You want to drive the nails?" Nathan rubbed his hands. They were already turning red and sore.

"Nah . . . hey!" Leah looked up with a wide grin. "Let's practice our lines for the play."

"Now?"

"Yeah. 'My maidens and I will fast too, and then I will' . . . 'I will' . . . Don't tell me. I'll get it. 'I will' . . . Aghhh! I never remember that line. I told Miss D'Imperio that I shouldn't have this part. Why did she make me Queen Esther? She knows I don't speak good."

"I don't like my part either," Colin yelled from the other end of a board. "Haman's not all that bad. I don't think it's fair that he gets hung!"

"Nathan, what comes after 'I will'?"

"'I will go to the king, which is—'"

"'Which is not permitted by the law,'" she squealed. "'And if . . . I perish, . . . I perish!'" She bowed low as she completed the line, which caused the weight of the board to shift to Colin, who promptly dropped it on his toe.

"Oh, man! Quit fooling around down there," he cried out. "I nearly broke my foot!"

"'The enemy is this wicked Haman!'" Leah grinned.

"It's not funny!" Colin called.

"Colin's right."

"I'm sorry, Colin," Leah apologized.

"Come on. Let's get this done and go buffalo hunting," Nathan encouraged them.

■

As it turned out, they ate the noon meal at Nathan's house. Then they mounted up for the ride out to the river with a flour sack stuffed with hay tied on the back of Onepenny. Tona trotted ahead of them.

When they arrived at the stage crossing, they searched the hillsides and cottonwoods but saw nothing.

"Maybe someone captured him," Leah suggested.

"Maybe the Indians shot him for food," Colin added.

"Yeah, and maybe he wandered off to find people who treat him nicer," Nathan replied. "Leah, you ride up on that bluff and see what you can see. Colin, you ride downstream. And I'll look upstream."

Within minutes, Colin screamed. Leah and Nathan raced to where Colin sat on his horse.

"There he is!" he shouted. "He's getting a drink!"

"What do we do now, Nathan?" Leah asked.

"Eh . . . you and Colin go way over by that tallest cotton-wood. When he comes out of the river, don't let him head that direction. Me and Onepenny will cut him off from this direction. Then he'll have to start moving toward town. I figure once we get him moving, we'll just hang way back and graze him toward town."

"So we just ride over there and wait for him to come back out of the river?" Leah asked.

"Yep. He surely can't stay in that one position very long," Nathan predicted.

Actually, according to Colin's pocket watch, Thunder stayed in the mud along the river for one hour and eleven minutes more. Nathan, Colin, and Leah were all under the same cottonwood tree, sprawled on a fallen log and studying every movement of the animal.

"I don't think he's leaving the mud," Colin said.

"Maybe we should throw something at him," Leah suggested.

Nathan paced in front of the other two. "No, that would aggravate him, and he'd charge right at us."

"Then see if you can get him to come out and eat some hay. Isn't that why you brought it?" she urged.

"I was saving it for an emergency," Nathan protested.

"Riggins, this is an emergency!" Colin hollered. "If we don't get him out of the river, we'll waste the whole afternoon."

"Okay. Take positions on both sides. Me and Onepenny will ride straight up to the bank of mud and scatter some hay."

When the other two were in position, Nathan rode toward the buffalo. Thunder stood at a forty-five-degree angle to the river. He could turn toward the water or glance back at the intruders. Most of the time he stared at Tona, who was content to bark at a considerable distance from everyone.

"Thunder! Look . . . it's your dinner! Come on, boy . . . come on! It's mighty good hay! Come on!" Nathan called.

The big bison glanced up at Nathan, still thirty feet away, and then stared at the hay on the river bank. Finally, he started to yank his right front foot out of the mud, but nothing happened. Over and over, the buffalo struggled to move one of his feet, but he remained rooted to that one position.

"He's stuck!" Leah called to Nathan.

"Man, we would have been waiting forever!" Colin griped. "Did you guys bring anything to eat? I'm hungry."

"Look, we are going to have to get him out."

"How?" Leah asked.

"Well . . . I'll . . . eh, I'll toss a loop over him and drag him out. I've seen them do that with cows."

"Didn't your daddy say not to rope him?" she protested.

"That's only when he's out running around. After we pull him out of the mud, he won't feel like running anywhere."

"Is your rope long enough to reach?" Colin asked.

"It is if I wade in there a little."

"Don't get Onepenny stuck," Leah warned.

Nathan pulled his rawhide *riata* off his saddle and made a big loop. He rotated the rope three times above his head and sailed the loop toward the buffalo's head.

The rope slapped up against the buffalo's nose, and the animal flipped it down in the mud.

"Almost, Nathan! Just a little further," Leah encouraged.

On the fourth attempt, the loop circled the buffalo's huge head, and Nathan pulled his end tight. The powerful animal jerked his neck back and almost yanked Nathan out of the saddle. Quickly he tied off the other end of the rope to his saddle horn.

"I'll just see if Onepenny can back him out of there. I'll keep at the end of the rope. When Thunder gets to the river bank where the hay is, he'll stop and eat. Then I'll see if I can flip the rope off."

Following Nathan's command, Onepenny began to back up the river bank until the rope stretched, strained, and groaned. But the buffalo didn't budge. Trying to avoid getting pinched between the tight rope and the saddle, Nathan spurred Onepenny up the river bank.

Just about the time he expected the rope to break, Leah let out a yell, "Keep going, Nathan! He's got a back leg loose!"

Then a front.

Then the other back.

Then a front.

And then the back ones were stuck again.

One step . . . tight rope . . . straining horse . . . slurping mud sounds . . . then another foot . . . then stuck again.

Very slowly, Thunder made his way to dry ground.

"You did it!" Leah shouted. "Nathan did it, Colin!"

Nathan, still almost thirty feet from the buffalo, struggled to untie the rope from his saddle horn. The buffalo in the meantime shook himself off like a dog after a bath, took one bite of the hay, and then, as if it were a sudden decision, bolted at full speed past a startled Nathan and Onepenny.

Frantically, Nathan still tried to untie the rope.

"Stay, Onepenny! Shut him down! You can hold him!"

The spotted horse dug his back feet into the soft ground

and shifted his weight back. When the buffalo hit the end of the rope, he had picked up full speed.

In an instant the cinch on Nathan's saddle snapped in two, and the whole saddle, with a panicked Nathan clutching the saddle horn, went flying into the air.

As he fell to the ground, he could hear Leah scream, "Turn loose! Nathan, turn loose!"

The warning wasn't needed. When he slammed into the ground, he lost his grip and rolled into the sagebrush. Staggering to his hands and knees, he watched as buffalo, rope, and saddle disappeared into the northern Nevada horizon.

3

Nathan!" Leah called as she rode toward him. "Nathan, are you hurt?"

With effort, he stood to his feet. His face felt fiery pain. There was a dull throb in his right leg, and a sharp pain shot through his arm. "I think I hit my elbow on a rock or something—that and scraping my face in the dirt . . . I'll be okay. Can you believe that he broke the cinch?"

"What do we do now?" Colin asked as he joined them.

"Go get my saddle back." Nathan dusted himself off and looked for his hat. "Where's Tona?"

"He was last seen chasing your saddle through the brush."

Nathan grabbed the reins on a waiting Onepenny. He spread out the maroon-and-black-striped Navajo saddle blanket, then grabbed a handful of the spotted horse's scraggly mane, and quickly pulled himself up on the horse.

"You goin' to ride bareback?" Colin asked.

"Until I find my saddle." He nodded.

"Where you learn to do that?" Leah asked.

"What?"

"Pull yourself up without a stirrup."

"A girl showed me."

"That Tashawna? Miss Show-off?"

"Nah, it was a Nez Percé girl named Eetalah. Why did you mention Tashawna . . . you aren't a little jealous, are you?"

"I ain't got one bit of jealous in me, and you know it, Nathan T. Riggins!"

Nathan kicked Onepenny, and they trotted off into the sage. A saddle dragged through the desert leaves a distinct trail, and they had no trouble finding the barking Tona and the buffalo. The shaggy-haired, short-horned, huge-headed, brown-eyed bison stood in a small meadow grazing on bunch grass and keeping one eye on Tona who still barked at the saddle.

"I'll try to get that rope untied," Nathan explained. "You two ride over by those rocks. That will give the buffalo something else to think about besides me."

Tona ran to his side when he climbed off Onepenny. Nathan could feel his boot heels sinking into the sandy prairie soil. Working quickly, with Thunder always in view, Nathan untied the rope and pulled back his gear.

The hay in the flour sack had scattered along the way, leaving a civilized trail in a primitive land. Nathan tied his saddle on the back of Leah's horse and remounted Onepenny.

"Now, let's move him toward town. He won't trot along like a cow, but we can graze him in that direction. Colin, you ride on the north side, and, Leah, you take the south. Give him about fifty feet and try not to make him angry."

"Where will you be?" Colin quizzed.

"Tona, Onepenny, and me will sweep along at the back. We'll be the ones to make him move. You two just keep him from drifting south or north."

"What about your rope?" Leah asked.

"I'll have to leave it until later."

With Leah and Colin in place, he rode Onepenny right at the buffalo. When they got within twenty feet, Thunder turned and stared at them. Nathan felt his stomach churn.

He's going to charge!

Then the buffalo looked back to the west and began to trot along through the sage.

"All right! That-a-boy, Onepenny. We bluffed him!" Nathan called.

Soon a pattern developed. The buffalo would wander about fifty steps in the general direction of town and then stop to eat grass and stare at his pursuers. Then Nathan would ride at him, which caused him to scoot on through the sage to another grassy morsel where he'd stop and repeat the process.

"This is getting really boring!" Colin hollered.

"Yeah, but it's working," Nathan called back.

"At this rate we won't get there until tomorrow."

"What's the rush? We've got all afternoon."

Leah held her hand up to shade her eyes. "Nathan, can I say my part in the play again?"

"Yeah . . . go ahead."

"Give me my cue."

Nathan held Onepenny back and let the buffalo eat. "Da te da te da . . . 'and who knows whether you have come to the kingdom for such a time as this?'"

Leah rolled her eyes toward the sky and spoke the words in a monotone, "'Go, gather together all the Jews in Shushan, and fast for me, and neither eat nor drink three days, night or day—'"

Then there was a long pause.

"Don't tell me!"

Nathan began to move the buffalo again.

"Oh, yeah! 'My maidens and I will fast too, and then I will go to the king . . . go to the king . . . to the king . . . the king.'"

"'WHICH IS NOT,'" Colin shouted. "For heaven's sake, Leah, we all know that line!"

"'Which is not permitted by the law; and if I perish, I perish!'" she stammered.

"Well, I'm going to perish at this speed," Colin complained. "I'll get him moving!" He turned his horse toward the buffalo and trotted right at him.

"Wait! Colin, no!" Nathan shouted waving his arms.

With sudden movement from the right, the buffalo stampeded to the left—right at Leah who was bowing in the saddle at the imaginary applause from her theater audience.

Her roan mare bolted at first sight of the charging buffalo. Leah tumbled off the back of the horse and bounced across the prairie.

Without hesitating, Nathan charged the buffalo. The animal veered to the west of Leah just enough to miss running right over the top of her.

"Colin, you idiot! Follow that buffalo!" Nathan shouted as he jumped down to the girl lying motionless next to the sage.

"Leah? Leah!" He knelt and tried to lift up her head. "Leah . . . are you all right? Leah? Say something!" Nathan pleaded. He gently brushed back her long brown hair.

One eye blinked opened and stared at Nathan. He saw her lips move, but he couldn't hear any words.

"What?" He leaned his ear close to her trembling lips.

Suddenly, she hollered, "I said, if I'm going to perish, I ain't going to perish fallin' off another horse!"

Nathan jumped back at her shout and dropped her head into the dirt.

"I'm sorry," he apologized.

Leah sat up and brushed off her dress. She sucked air and tried to talk. "Nathan T. Riggins, I'm going home. Every time I ride out with you, I get dumped. It's hard to be ladylike when I keep falling off a horse."

35

"Yeah . . . maybe we've done enough for one day."

"Done enough? We've only moved him two miles closer to town."

"At this rate we'll get him there in just five more days," Nathan calculated.

"I ain't got that many arms and legs to break, and you ain't got that many saddles."

"I'm not giving up. I just got to figure a different tactic."

"Yeah, and next time it won't involve me!" she insisted.

Nathan led Onepenny and walked Leah across the prairie to where her horse was standing. She stooped over with her hands on her hips, still trying to regain her pattern of breathing. He left her standing and crawled up on Onepenny.

"Wait here and rest. I'll go get Colin. Then we'll go back to town."

Nathan rode through the sage following the hoof prints of Colin's horse. The hot spring sun glared off the hillside in the breezeless afternoon. He was surprised at how far the buffalo had run. He grabbed tight to Onepenny's mane as they worked their way down a steep *barranca* and along an almost dry streambed. Then the track crossed the little creek and climbed a sheer bank on the far side. Nathan had to pull back on the reins to keep Onepenny from running up the incline. Even before Nathan made it to the top, he could hear Tona's barking.

Cresting the ridge, Nathan was surprised to see a small one-room cabin that was leaning so much it looked as if it would collapse at any moment.

Colin was on his horse facing the building about fifty feet away. Tona was close to the open door barking with unceasing fury.

"Where's Thunder?" Nathan yelled.

"In the cabin," Colin replied.

"Inside? You're kidding me!"

"Look. See your rope coming out the doorway? I saw him run right into that cabin."

"What's he doing in there?"

"How should I know? Maybe he's cooking supper. I'm sure not going in to find out! How's Leah?"

"She's all right . . . eh . . . we're going back to town."

"Giving up on the buffalo? Now that's the smartest thing you've decided in—"

"I'm not giving up! I just want to figure a better method."

"Yeah . . . whatever. Just make sure the next plans don't involve me," Colin replied.

Nathan slid down off Onepenny. "I'm going up to take a look at what he's doing."

"On foot?"

"Yeah. Is that all right with you?"

"Sure, I'll just scrape up what's left of you and carry it back to your mother in a bucket."

Nathan ignored the comment and slowly approached the cabin. He noticed that the door was off the hinges and lying across the front porch, which consisted mainly of broken boards.

The rear end of the buffalo was in full sight, but Nathan couldn't see the head of the animal. As he approached Tona, the dog quit barking and waited by his side. Taking one step at a time, Nathan watched for any sign of movement and tried to keep his spurs from jingling.

If he turns for that doorway, I'm running! Lord, keep me from doing something really, really dumb.

Nathan walked all the way to the porch before he could see the whole animal. For several minutes he just stared.

"What's he doing?" Colin yelled from his position of safety.

"He's just licking the dirt."

"What?"

"He's just licking the dirt. You know, the cabin has a dirt floor, and he's in there licking it."

"Buffaloes don't eat dirt!"

"No, not eating . . . licking. You know, like a salt block? That's it! I'll bet that's a salt lick! You know, where the mineral content's real high! I read about those one time."

"He's really just licking the dirt?"

"Yep." Then Nathan turned to go back to Onepenny. As he did, he slapped his leg and called, "Okay, Tona!" Suddenly, the dog flew into an outrage of barking and dove through the open doorway after the buffalo.

"Tona! No!" Nathan screamed. "I didn't mean attack! I meant come on, let's go home! Tona!"

There was a rumble, a snort, and an explosive crashing of timber as the buffalo butted his way right through the end of the building. Boards and splinters flew everywhere, and Tona was at the big animal's heels.

Nathan jumped back. With a loud crash the entire cabin collapsed into a rubble of broken boards and fractured shingles.

Colin rode up leading Onepenny.

"Did you see that?" Nathan shouted. "Did you see that? He brought the whole building down!"

"We better go catch Tona before he chases that buffalo all the way back to—"

"Hey," Nathan interrupted, "that's the direction of town, isn't it? Let's go get Leah, and then we'll see how far they run."

Nathan and Colin rode back across the prairie, down across the creekbed, to the place they had left Leah.

"Where is she? Did she go home already?" Colin asked.

"Leah? Hey . . . where are you?"

A panicked feeling hit Nathan as he looked down at the tracks in the dirt.

"She probably went—," Colin began.

"Look! Look at those tracks! Someone rode by here . . . no, there were two of them . . . then three. They took Leah with them! They're headed east. Galena is west."

"Maybe they were friends of hers," Colin offered.

"We're friends of hers. She wouldn't desert us. I can't believe I left her out here."

Dropping the reins, Nathan stood straight up on the saddle blanket.

"Can you see her?" Colin pressed.

"I think there's some movement over across the prairie, but it might just be a dust devil. Colin, you ride back to Galena and tell my dad what happened. I'm going to follow this trail."

"What about Tona?"

"He'll take care of himself."

"What about the buffalo?"

"Forget the buffalo. We have to find Leah!"

Nathan clutched Onepenny's mane and kicked the pony's sides as they loped down the trail of the three horses.

Lord, I don't understand. I mean, she was winded, so I just left her there for a minute to go get Colin . . . how could she? . . . Lord, I keep getting Leah into tough situations. It's not fair. She shouldn't even be out here! She's just got to be all right! Please, Lord.

The tracks made a sharp left turn and headed straight toward the mountains. He wiped the sweat from his forehead and replaced his hat.

I've got to find her before we reach the mountains. I can't go in there alone.

Nathan kicked Onepenny into a gallop. It was all he could do to hold on and not get bounced off. The horse slammed into his backside like a paddle during a spanking. Then he saw a grove of cottonwoods tucked up against the hills—and a stout set of corrals with fifteen to twenty horses milling in various pens. He was surprised no one was with the horses.

Horse thieves? Maybe they stole Leah's horse. Maybe they shot her and left her back there on the prairie!

A well-worn trail stretched away from the corrals back up into a canyon. The entry was narrow, and Nathan felt as if he were entering a trap. He slowly rode Onepenny deeper into the shadows. A cool, comfortable breeze drifted out of the canyon, and Nathan could smell sweet grass somewhere up ahead. Finally, the trail broke into an open meadow covered with green grass and purple wildflowers.

He stopped the horse the minute he spotted the small log cabin at the back of the meadow. It stood against a massive sandstone cliff, and a thin trail of smoke feathered skyward from the chimney. Nathan thought he could see three horses tied in front. One was Leah's roan mare. He left Onepenny grazing back in the shadows and crept through the tall grass on his hands and knees.

My saddle is still on Leah's horse . . . if I can sneak up close and pull my rifle . . . maybe . . . Lord, please don't let anything happen to Leah.

A natural spring seeped into the middle of the meadow, and Nathan soon was dragging himself through mud.

I've got to get there quickly . . . really quick!

Once he reached the yard, Nathan crouched behind a stubby tree and looked for movement in the cabin. Then he crept over to Leah's horse. Carefully standing up so the horse would block the view of anyone in the cabin, Nathan quietly unsnapped his rifle from the scabbard. Creeping up to the front porch, he crawled under the unshuttered window. Nathan held his rifle toward the door as he strained to hear what was going on inside. He could hear muffled voices and whispers, but they seemed to be coming from a back room.

Lord, I'm just a kid. What if I run in there, and they just shoot me down? Then I haven't helped Leah at all. And what if I don't? What if she needs me right now?

Suddenly, the front door opened. Nathan threw the gun to his shoulder, but he had no idea what he would do next. No one appeared at the door, but a brown ball of fur tumbled out onto the porch, and the door was once again slammed shut. The little fur ball jumped to its feet, yipped once at Nathan, and then trotted over to him.

A puppy? These horse thieves keep a puppy in there?

The pup excitedly sniffed Nathan's boots.

Tona! He smells Tona!

Nathan reached down and scratched the little dog's head. The big-footed, flop-eared pup rolled over on its back.

"You want your stomach scratched, huh, boy?" Nathan whispered. "I wish you could tell me what's going on in there."

The pup crawled up on Nathan's lap and settled down, closing his eyes in the warm afternoon sun. Nathan petted the dog a few more times and then set the sleeping puppy on the front porch. Slowly, Nathan pulled himself up to the window, hoping to get a quick peek inside.

Just as he got his left eye even with the glass window, he spotted a kid with his face to the window looking out at him. In panic, Nathan fell to the porch and scurried around to the side of the building.

He saw me for sure! They've got some other kid in there and . . .

Then he had a sinking feeling—the kind he always got in

class when he went to the chalkboard to do a problem and everyone in class could see him do it wrong.

It was me! Riggins, you idiot, that was your reflection in the glass! Oh, man, I hope nobody ever finds out about this.

The puppy had trailed him around to the side and stayed underfoot as he made his way back to the front porch. He had just about gotten up enough nerve to peek through the window again when an agonizing scream echoed out of the back room.

Nathan jumped to his feet, cocked his rifle, and kicked open the front door. He burst through the dimly lit, unoccupied front room and barged into the back room waving his rifle and shouting, "Leah! Leah!"

He stopped immediately in his tracks when he saw what was happening in the room.

"Leah? Dr. Stanton? Oh no . . . that lady in bed . . . she's having a . . . a . . ."

"Nathan T. Riggins, you get out of here right now," Leah scolded. "Cain't you see she's having a baby! Go on! Go on!"

"Horse thieves . . . where's the horse . . . it's a real baby!"

The voices sounded distant to Nathan, and all in the room looked as if they were standing far away at the end of a tunnel. Above a dull hum, Nathan heard Leah yell, "Don't you go fainting on us, Nathan Riggins. Doc Stanton and me is busy enough with tending to a . . ."

Then everything went black.

4

*T*he voices were familiar. A man
. . . a woman . . . another man . . . a girl. The girl was talking
to him. But it was dark. And she spoke softly. Persistently.

Nathan knew he should be saying something.

But he couldn't remember where he was.

Leah!

He sat straight up opening both eyes wide.

"Leah?"

"Well, if it ain't the world's bravest boy! It's a good thing
Doc Stanton didn't need you to help out. When it comes to
deliverin' babies, you're 'bout as valuable as a sack of taters!"

"Baby? That lady was having a baby!" Nathan looked
around and realized he was now in the front room of the cabin.

"That lady is Mrs. Dodge, and you sure didn't help none
runnin' in there waving a gun and shoutin'! What was you
yelling about?"

"Horse thieves . . . I mean . . . I thought you'd been kidnapped or something."

"And you was comin' to rescue me?" Leah asked.

"Eh . . . well . . . yeah, I guess that was it."

"Well, I was waiting out there for you and Colin, and all
of a sudden Doc Stanton and Mr. Dodge come galloping along.
Doc shouts to follow him cause he's going to need my help."

"You?"

"I helped him deliver Mrs. McNeil's baby last December, or don't you remember?"

"Eh . . . I guess I forgot."

"Well, Mrs. Dodge was havin' a real tough time with a breech birth, and so Mr. Dodge rode for the Doc, and I came to help."

"But you're just a girl—a kid . . . you don't . . ."

"I know a whole lot more things than you think I know, Mr. Nathan T. Riggins!"

"How about the baby? Is he . . . eh, she . . . is it all right?"

"*He* is doing very well, thank you. Christopher Carson Dodge. But Mrs. Dodge is pretty much worn out. Doc Stanton has to get on out to the Konesky's, so they asked if I would spend the night here. Just in case I could be some help."

"Really? They want you?"

Leah tilted her head and let slip a half-grin, half-frown. There was something about the expression that startled Nathan.

It's like Leah . . . but it's not Leah. It's . . . it's like an older Leah. It's like she isn't a kid anymore.

"Nathan?"

"Uh . . . yeah?"

"You was starin' at me."

"Oh . . . maybe . . . you know, I'm still a little fuzzy from fainting."

"Well, I need you to tell my daddy that I'll probably be here until after dinner tomorrow. Then I'll ride back."

"By yourself?"

"You could come out and ride back with me if you want, but I ain't afraid to ride by myself, mind ya."

"Yeah . . . after church I'll come out." Nathan stood to his feet and picked up his rifle and his hat.

Doctor Stanton came out of the room with Mr. Dodge and left some final instructions for Leah.

"Well, son," he said resting his hand on Nathan's shoulder, "I think we can leave now."

"Yes, sir, I'm sorry for barging in there like that, Mr. Dodge. I was looking for Leah."

"No problem, son. I'd have acted the same way if I thought my Sarah was in danger. You got a mighty fine girlfriend here. She's a stander. If I was you, I'd keep the other boys away from her, if you catch my drift." Mr. Dodge grinned.

"Well, he ain't my—," Leah began.

"Yes, sir, I think I will," Nathan interrupted.

He borrowed a cinch from Mr. Dodge, and Leah walked with him across the meadow to where Onepenny stood munching on the grass. As he repaired his saddle, Leah asked, "Did you really break in there thinking you'd have to shoot your way out to rescue me?"

"Yeah."

"Thanks. You're a good friend. I ain't never had many friends that good. I mean, I ain't never had *any* friend that good."

"Well, a person's got to stick by his friends—right?"

"Yeah." Leah watched Nathan mount up and stand in the stirrups to get the saddle well set. "Nathan, you know, if you wanted to . . . I mean, if you ever needed to say to someone that you was my boyfriend, I promise I won't get mad at you."

Nathan smiled. "Okay, but I better not tell old Kylie Collins that."

"Now jist 'cause I said you can call me your girlfriend don't mean I'm goin' to marry you!"

"Here comes Doc. I'll see you tomorrow." He turned toward the oncoming horse and spurred Onepenny. Just when he reached the rocky, narrow exit of the canyon, he turned and waved to Leah, who still stood shading her eyes by the cottonwood.

She waved back.

When they reached the horse corrals, Doc Stanton stopped and let his horse drink from the springs.

"Well, Nathan, you head on back to town. I've got one more stop to make."

"Doc, what's with this pen of wild horses?"

"Well, Mr. Dodge breaks horses for the army up at Fort Hall. And he says there isn't enough water for them all up in the canyon, so he leaves them down here unless he expects some trouble. You'll talk to Mr. Walker for me, won't you? I don't want him worrying about Leah."

"I'll go tell him."

"Well, I'll see you back in town."

"Yes, sir."

After watching Doctor Stanton ride out of sight, Nathan returned to the prairie and took the stage road back to Galena. It was a good half-hour before he remembered Colin. *Oh no! I told Colin to send my dad out with some men to rescue Leah! He'll be riding out here for nothing.*

Nathan spurred Onepenny to a fast trot and pulled his stampede string tight against his chin. Expecting to spot his dad at every rise and turn, he was surprised when he caught sight of Galena in the distance.

"Maybe I missed him," he moaned to his spotted horse.

He was planning on riding straight to his father's office, but a noise off in the sage to the left caught his attention.

"Tona? Hey, Tona!"

Nathan jumped down to grab his gray and white dog.

"You just came on home? That's a good boy! What are you barking at? My rope! All right! You drug my rope all the way home?"

Nathan grabbed the end of the rope and began to coil it neatly.

"We'll go back out tomorrow afternoon and get that old boy. I think he'll move for us if we catch him in a good mood. Hey, you must have caught this on a . . . sage . . . oh, no!"

Nathan had rounded the tall sagebrush, and suddenly he was not more that ten feet away from 2,500 pounds of very tired buffalo. Thunder, still wearing Nathan's rope like a necktie, lay in the dirt, lathered up and panting.

"Eh, excuse me . . . I think I'll just . . . walk on back out of here," Nathan stammered.

At a safe distance Nathan remounted Onepenny and circled the beast.

"Tona, did you run him all the way to town? I don't believe it! Did Colin help you? He probably kept you going toward town, didn't he? Where is Colin? I bet he rode on in to get Dad. I told him to forget about the buffalo. Anyway, come on Tona; we can let that old boy rest awhile."

Nathan rode straight to his dad's office and explained the situation with Leah. He was surprised to find out that Colin hadn't come by yet.

"He was awful hungry," Nathan added as he left the marshal's office. "Maybe he went over to the Mercantile to buy some of those creme fills."

Nathan stopped by Mr. Walker's barber shop and told Leah's father where she was. Then he swung by the Mercantile, but no one had seen Colin.

Did he go home for supper without even sending anyone out to help me and Leah? What if there really had been trouble? What if we had been kidnapped by horse thieves? What if we were shot and bleeding in some lonely cabin? What if the Indians carried us off to make us slaves in their secret camp?

What if . . . Lord, I've got to stop reading all those stories in Frank Leslie's Illustrated.

Nathan picked up a fresh sack of hay at the Lander County Livery and rode by the Shipley place.

"Well, Tona, our corral sure looks stout enough. I guess we'll know soon enough."

Nathan took about six trips to the Shipley well with an iron-handled wooden bucket and filled a small water trough in the corral. Then he opened the gate wide and propped it that way with a rock. He crawled back up on Onepenny.

"Now if Mr. Thunder will just march into that pen, I'll have me my buffalo."

And if he doesn't, he'll probably stampede through town terrorizing every man, woman, and child. . . . I ought to go find Colin and make him help me finish this job. But if I can do it myself, I bet no one else in this whole town ever penned a buffalo single-handed.

As he rode back out of town, he noticed a wagon stopped out in the sagebrush near where he had left the buffalo. When he came closer, he could read the faded sign on the side—Hawthorne H. Miller, Photographer, Author, Lecturer. He was startled to see the wagon parked not more than twenty-five feet from the buffalo. Thunder gawked warily at a man in dirty gray frock coat moving quickly to set up his equipment. He hummed and sang as he worked.

"'Tenting tonight, tenting tonight, tenting on the old camp ground . . . '"

"Excuse me, Mister."

"Oh . . . my word, you startled me, son. I'm terribly busy at the moment. Just wait 'til I'm through. Say, maybe you'd like to help me. Could you hand me that black box, the little one there."

Still mounted on Onepenny, Nathan lifted the box out of the wagon and handed it to the man.

"Mister, you better be careful. That—"

"Son, I know exactly what I'm doing. You are speaking to none other than Hawthorne H. Miller! I'm sure you've read my books and seen some of my photographic exhibits."

"I've never heard of you."

"Oh . . . well, I suppose things are primitive out here. Ah, so much the better. More people will be delighted to purchase such historic photographs."

"Mr. Miller, I'm not joshing you. If that buffalo decides to run, he'll bust your camera, your wagon, and your body like it was a matchstick."

"Well, he looks rather docile. Besides, I tied the end of that rope to the wagon wheel. Just how far can he get?"

"A wagon wheel? He'll rip that off and drag it all the way to Utah."

"I hardly think so." Miller pushed his rounded crown hat back and glanced up at Nathan sitting in the saddle. "What makes you an expert on buffalo?"

"I'm not an expert. But Thunder there is my buffalo."

"What do you mean, your buffalo? People don't own buffaloes."

"I do. That's my rope on him, and I've got a bill of sale right here in my pocket. I bought Thunder from Dakota Williams."

"Dakota Williams!" Miller roared. "Thunder? This is the famous buffalo, Thunder? My word, I saw him at the Rocky Mountain Exposition in North Platte last fall!"

"Well, he belongs to me now, and I can't let you take a picture of him."

"Hmphh. I suppose you want a sitting fee. It's an outrage,

but I'll . . . I'll give you fifty cents for permission to photograph the buffalo."

"Nope, I don't want—"

"Oh, my word, is there no respect for art? Money-hungry children just don't . . . oh, all right. One dollar, but not a copper more. Do you understand?"

"Mr. Miller, you can't photograph him right now for all the money in the Comstock. I've got to get him into a corral in town first. Then you can photograph him for free. If you flash that pan, he'll run off, and I'll have to start all over."

"Obviously, you know very little about this buffalo. Thunder was raised as an infant by Dakota Williams and used to eat scraps at the family table. I read it in the broadside advertisement for the Exposition. Look at him! You could probably get him to roll over and let you scratch his stomach. Say? I wonder if you'd like to be in the picture? You could—"

"I'm not getting close to him, Mr. Miller. I don't care what you read in some flyer—he's about as wild and stubborn as they come. He's charged me on more than one occasion, and I just saw him level a cabin about five miles down the road. Like I said, as soon as I get him penned, I'll let you photograph him through the gate or something."

"Corral? Penned? Anyone can photograph a buffalo in captivity, but out here in the wild—what a shot! 'The Last Buffalo in Nevada!' Tremendous! Splendid!"

Miller returned to setting up his equipment.

"Mr. Miller, you can't do it. I won't let you do it. He's my buffalo, and you can't go scaring him off!"

"Son, you annoy me. If you persist in being distractive, you leave me no choice but to report you to the local constable."

"You mean the marshal in Galena?"

"Is that the name of this town?"

"Yes, sir."

"Well, then, I will surely report you to the marshal of Galena!"

Nathan reached over and pulled his rifle out of the scabbard.

"I s-say," Miller stammered, "no young ruffian will threaten me!"

"How about going to get the marshal? Tell him his son, Nathan, won't let you scare off his buffalo."

"Your father is the marshal? My word, what kind of town is this?"

"Look, Mr. Miller, I really don't want you to scare the buffalo. So just pack up your gear and slip out of here before he makes kindling out of you and your wagon."

The man stared at Nathan for a long moment. Then he shrugged. "Well, if that's your decision . . . of course it will take me a few moments to break it all back down."

"I'm sorry, but it's just got to be that way."

Miller fumbled with some of the gear and then put the little black box back into the wagon.

"'Tenting tonight, tenting tonight, tenting on the old camp ground,'" he sang.

Nathan watched the buffalo intently. He thought Thunder was about to make a move. When the massive bison lifted his head, Nathan called out, "Watch out, Mr. Miller. He's getting up!"

"Splendid!" Miller called and ducked under the black canvas at the rear of the camera.

Nathan glanced at the standing buffalo and backed Onepenny away from the wagon.

"Mr. Miller, get out of there!" he hollered.

Then it dawned on him what Miller was doing.

"No!" Nathan yelled.

Black powder flashed.

Nathan held his breath.

Thunder charged.

Hawthorne H. Miller, with terror in his eyes, dove back under his wagon. The two mules hitched to the wagon panicked and attempted to pull away Miller's hiding place. Thunder clipped the side of the camera, jumped over Miller, and headed for the open prairie.

At least the rope will break!

It didn't.

Instead, the spokes of the wagon wheel snapped like dry twigs, and the huge metal rim bounced like an anchor following the buffalo. The photographer's wagon overturned, and the mules halted. To Nathan's surprise, Thunder ran about a hundred steps out on the prairie and then stopped.

"Mr. Miller, are you all right? Are you hurt?" Nathan slid off Onepenny and ran to the man still crouching in the dirt.

"My word, the animal's a killer! My plates! Did he break the plates?" He rushed to the toppled camera. "They're still intact! I must hurry. I must hurry. Charging buffalo! Oh, splendid. Yes . . . yes. Hurry, son, help me set up my dark tent. I'll need to develop this and . . . well, don't just stand there! Get me my large valise!"

"Mr. Miller, I'm going to try to get my buffalo into a pen. You can do anything you want."

Miller seemed to ignore both Nathan and the recent near disaster. "'Tenting tonight, tenting tonight, tenting on the old campground,'" he sang as he packed his camera over to the tipped wagon.

Nathan mounted his horse and trotted out to Thunder. The animal took several steps away from him, but the weight of the wagon wheel caused him to stop again.

"Tona, I don't think he can go too fast dragging that wheel. Let's keep him moving toward town."

With Tona barking, Onepenny and Nathan put continual pressure on the buffalo. The huge beast reluctantly retreated closer and closer to the Shipley corral and the open gate.

By taking it slow and allowing the animal plenty of rest stops, Nathan maneuvered the buffalo right next to the corral gate. But try as he might, Nathan couldn't get the buffalo to walk in. Every time he put on a little pressure, Nathan could see the animal searching for a direction to run back to the prairie.

"Tona, if we push him, he'll run away. Maybe I'll leave you and Onepenny here and go scatter some hay in the corral. Perhaps he'll go for the hay."

Nathan debated in his mind the wisdom of crawling off his horse this close to the buffalo. As he was still thinking about it, Tona ducked under the bottom rail of the corral and put his front paws on the water trough. Still keeping an eye on the buffalo, the dog began to lap water.

Hearing the noise of the dog drinking, the big buffalo spun toward the gate opening and trotted right into the corral and over to the water.

"Tona! You did it!" Nathan jumped off Onepenny and quickly closed the gate and slid a four-by-four board into the locked position.

The dog hustled out of the corral. Nathan untied the wagon wheel, which still lay outside the gate. He lifted it up and rolled it over to the fence, leaning it against a rail.

"I don't know how I'm going to get that rope off," he mumbled to Tona.

He gazed through the rails at the enormous animal as it slurped the water. Then he grabbed the sack of hay and dumped it over the fence into the corral. When the buffalo had his fill, he backed away from the trough, shook his head violently back and forth, flipping the rope to the ground. Then he began to chomp on the hay.

Nathan retrieved his rope by pulling it under the rail of the corral and was tying it back to his saddle horn when Mr. Maddison walked up to him.

"Well, I see you boys herded up that buffalo after all!"

"Yes, sir." Nathan beamed.

"Well, he's a majestic animal. Did you name him?"

"Dakota Williams called him Thunder, so I'm just going to keep that name."

"Sounds good to me. He's the only buffalo in Nevada. Where did Colin go? I told his mother I'd send him on home, and I can't seem to locate him."

"Well, he came on in before me. We sort of . . . well, it's a long story. Anyway, he was supposed to go see my dad, but he didn't. So he's either at home or down at the Mercantile sampling those creme fills."

"I just left the Mercantile and the house. He's not at either place. And his horse isn't back at the livery. I thought for sure he was with you."

"You mean, Colin hasn't it made it back to town yet?" Nathan glanced back out at the prairie. "I really thought he could find his way back."

5

As he and Mr. Maddison scurried through Galena looking for Colin, Nathan related the whole story of the buffalo roundup, Leah's disappearance, and Colin's return for help. But although they looked everywhere, they found no trace of Colin.

"Mr. Maddison, I don't kn-know what to say," Nathan stammered. "We were just across the creek from the Galena road. I know Colin couldn't have missed it. Besides, he's a good rider. I came up that road myself, and I didn't see him."

"You're right." Mr. Maddison took a deep breath and sighed. "He's quite capable of getting himself home from there. That's the problem. Who else did you see on the road?"

"Well . . . there were a couple freight wagons . . . and a photographer—Mr. Hawthorne Miller. That was his rig out by the Shipley place."

"I'll get my horse and check with Miller. Nathan, I'll need you to ride out with me and show me where you saw Colin last. It could be he's just lost."

"Yes, sir. I'm going to tell Dad. Maybe he can come with us."

"Yes, please do that!"

Mr. Maddison scrambled toward the livery as Nathan dashed for his father's office. In a matter of minutes, Marshal

Riggins, Mr. Maddison, and Nathan were riding out of Galena.

"David, I really appreciate your coming out with me." Mr. Maddison nodded. "It could be just a dawdling youth."

"Nothing would make me happier," Mr. Riggins replied. "It seems strange he would lose his way so close to town."

It was thirty minutes later when Marshal Riggins stopped the other two.

"You see that trail? A wagon rolled across here this afternoon heading north, and it had a horse tied to the rear. See that extra set of prints?"

"Could that be Colin's horse?" Nathan asked.

"No tellin'. This main road has had too many wagons and horses today to be able to distinguish any one track. If we don't find anything better, then we'll come back and take a look at this."

When they finally reached the river crossing, the marshal made a troubling discovery.

"Indians. Maybe a dozen . . . one lodge . . . see where the travois poles drug in the dirt?"

"Indians?" Mr. Maddison choked. "We don't have any Indians around here . . . do we?"

"Not normally. They usually keep themselves up at Ft. McDermitt or at Duck Valley, but they were obviously here."

"I met some Shoshone Indians out here somewhere last year," Nathan recalled. "I think the chief's name was Pie-a-ra-poo'-na. He had a young Nez Percé girl with him named Eetahla."

"You saw Indians out here today?" Mr. Maddison asked.

"No, that was last year. I didn't see any Indians today."

Marshal Riggins turned his horse up the trail to follow the Indian sign.

"I say, David, is it advisable to follow the Shoshone?" Mr. Maddison questioned.

"If it were my boy, I'd follow them even if they were the James gang!"

"Yes . . . yes, you're quite right." Mr. Maddison pulled a snub-nosed Colt out of his coat and spun the chambers.

"Now we aren't lookin' for trouble. Colin might not be with them at all," the marshal cautioned.

"I can't see any trail of a shoed horse," Nathan complained to his father.

"Nope. I don't see one either. But I do see that the travois is rigged in such a way as to brush out tracks. So we'll follow this trail for a while anyway."

Marshal Riggins led the way, leaning over in the saddle to study the signs in the dirt. Mr. Maddison rode next, keeping his eyes on the horizon looking for riders . . . or one particular rider. Nathan rode last. When his father wasn't watching, he slipped his rifle out of the scabbard and laid it across his lap.

The air was perfectly still—the sky clear. Nathan could hear nothing except the soft plodding hoofs on the Nevada dirt and the occasional squeak of saddle leather or the tinkle of a jingle-bob on his spur.

They had just reached the top of the first hill when they saw a teepee rigged up next to a tiny creek. Several people were around a fire that burned in front of the lodge. A dozen horses milled nearby.

"Do you see Colin?" Mr. Maddison asked nervously.

"Nope. But they see us. Three of them are standing on this side of the fire toting guns. We might as well ride in."

"Will there be shooting?" Mr. Maddison asked.

"I would certainly hope not," the marshal replied.

Three Indian men, packing rifles, met them at the edge of camp.

"We are looking for a lost boy," Marshal Riggins called out. "Have you seen him out here anywhere?"

The Indian with the barrel chest answered, "A white boy?"

"Yes."

"How big?"

"Just about this boy's size." He pointed to Nathan.

"I will ask."

He turned to speak to the others and then walked back into the teepee.

Suddenly a young girl darted out of the lodge and ran their way.

"Nathan!"

"Eetahla! Father, this is the girl I was telling you about."

"You found your mother and father?" she asked him.

"Yes . . . eh, you didn't get to go back to your people?" Nathan quizzed.

"No, but I am happy. Did you come to carry me off?" she teased.

"No," Nathan joked, "I'm not rich enough yet."

"But you have a beautiful pony. He is one of ours—a Nez Percé horse."

"Yes, I know, and his name is Onepenny."

"Did you know that I have a new name?" She beamed.

"What's wrong with Eetahla? It's a very pretty name."

"Yes, but I was given another name when I was baptized."

"Baptized?" Nathan questioned.

"Yes, yes, it was very exciting. We wintered near Ft. Hall, and a Bibleman and his family were also wintering there. He came to our lodge often and told us about God and Jesus and the Holy Ghost."

"And you were baptized?"

"Yes, many of this band were baptized. He gave me my very own Bible, and as soon as I learn to read, I am going to study it."

About this time the young man emerged from the teepee and returned to Marshal Riggins.

"None of us saw a boy. However, there were two men in a wagon trying to sell us very poor goods. Perhaps they saw the boy."

"What men?"

"White men with little round hats and soft hands. They had broken muzzle-loading guns, worn-out blankets, and whiskey. We would not trade with them for those things. They were very angry and threatened to shoot us with their revolvers."

"What did you do?" Mr. Maddison asked.

"We took away their bullets." The Indian smiled showing a tooth missing. "We gave them an old buffalo robe for all their bullets. It was a very good trade."

"Where did you last see them?"

"Near the buffalo cabin."

"Buffalo cabin?" Marshal Riggins asked.

"I know where it is!" Nathan shouted. "That's where Thunder found a salt lick and tore down a whole cabin!"

"Well, lead us there."

Then the marshal turned to the Indians.

"Listen," he said to the spokesman, "it was reported that a herd of pronghorn antelope are just north of here near Three Bear Mountain."

The Indian quickly translated the words to the others.

"That is very good news!" He nodded. "If we see the boy you are looking for, we will make him go home."

"I'd appreciate it," Mr. Maddison responded as he turned his horse to leave.

Eetahla stood next to Nathan's horse. "If we find the boy, I will make sure he is safe."

"Thanks." Nathan smiled. "I'm glad you were baptized."

"Yes, and next time you must let me ride Onepenny!" she shouted as he turned and waved good-bye.

When they were out of sight of the Indians, Colin's father asked, "Do you believe them?"

"The Indians?"

"Yes."

"Yep. There was no reason for them to lie."

"What about those traders?"

"Obviously some riffraff that just got off the train from the East. It wouldn't hurt to check them out—providing we can find them."

Nathan led them to the now-destroyed cabin on the salt lick, and they rode ever-widening concentric circles around the cabin until they found wagon tracks.

"That's what I thought. These are the same tracks that crossed the Galena road."

"Where are the horse tracks?" Nathan asked. "You said there was a horse tied to the back of the wagon."

"You're right, Nate. There's no horse tied to it here. Let's follow these wagon tracks!" Marshal Riggins spurred his horse, and the other two followed down the dusty trail through the sage.

The shadows from the horses stretched long to the east, and Nathan figured they had no more than an hour of daylight left when they plodded up a mountainous draw leading to a clump of piñon pine trees. They would have to turn around very soon to make it back to the Galena road before dark.

Within a couple hundred yards of the trees, the marshal stopped. "Nathan, if we are following someone who doesn't want to be followed, then that grove of trees is where they will make a stand. You stay here. If you hear shooting, I want you and Onepenny to race to Galena. Get Deputy Hailey to round up a half-dozen good men and then come back out here—even if it's dark. Have you got that?"

"Yes, sir. I'll stay right here unless I hear shooting or you signal me up."

Nathan slipped down off Onepenny and readjusted his saddle. Then he walked the horse out away from the sage so that he could see his father and Mr. Maddison from where he stood on the trail. He glanced at them, then at the small grove of trees up the draw, and then at the surrounding countryside. What he saw was mile after mile of sagebrush, treeless high-desert basin, rolling hills, and a few jagged mountains.

It all looks the same . . . Austin . . . Eureka . . . Galena . . . Elko . . . Wells Station . . . White Pine . . . it's just Nevada—that's all.

Lord, I'm really worried about Colin. I shouldn't have let him . . . but I really thought . . . Lord, don't let anything happen to Colin, please!

As Nathan saw the men approach the grove of trees, he remounted Onepenny.

"We'd better be ready to ride, boy." He patted the spotted horse's neck, which felt warm and moist.

Suddenly, he heard a voice–shrill, distant, and obviously anxious. It sent a chill right down Nathan's back.

"Nathan!" He heard it a second time.

He spun in the saddle and pulled his rifle from the scabbard.

"Nathan! Over here!"

His gaze searched the horizon, bouncing off green hills and gray sage, but he couldn't locate the voice. "Colin?"

"The rock! Behind the two rocks!"

About a hundred yards away, Nathan noticed a granite

outcropping of rocks almost concealed by tall sagebrush. He spun Onepenny in that direction and trotted toward the voice. As he approached the rocks, Colin's hatless head popped up from behind the rocks. "Don't come any closer!" he shouted.

Nathan reined up. "Colin, are you all right?" he called.

"Yeah . . . not really . . . well, sort of!"

"What?" Nathan began to ride around the rock.

"Stay there!" Colin shouted.

"Why? What's going on?" Nathan could only see Colin's head appearing above the rocks.

"Well, I had a little trouble on my way back to Galena. You see, I met these two traders—at least they claimed to be traders—in a wagon. They said they had some goods I might be interested in."

"But it was a bunch of junk, right?"

"Yeah. Did you see them too?" Colin questioned.

"Nope, but the Indians mentioned them."

"Indians? You mean there're Indians out here?"

"Colin, go on; what happened?" Nathan prodded.

"Well, naturally, I wasn't about to trade for inferior merchandise, and I told them so."

"That didn't make them real happy, did it?"

"No. They were quite indignant. One of them insisted on having my woolly chaps. When I refused and began to ride off, they grabbed my horse and forced me to come with them."

"Where did they take you?"

"Up to that grove of cottonwoods."

"Then what happened?"

"Then," Colin fumed, "they stole my horse, my saddle, my chaps, my boots . . . and my other personal items. They rode off laughing, leaving me in the trees."

"Other personal items?" Nathan questioned. "You mean, like your shirt, suspenders, and britches?"

"Precisely."

"You mean they left you in the grove wearing nothing but your underwear?"

"They left me, Riggins, wearing nothing but my birthday suit!" Colin said angrily.

"You mean you're completely . . ."

"I mean you had better toss me that blanket rolled up on your cantle."

Nathan untied the blanket behind his saddle. For a split second he considered tossing it short of the rocks and making Colin sneak out for it. Instead, he threw it over the rocks, and soon the blanket-wrapped figure emerged.

"Did they beat you up or hurt you?" Nathan asked.

"No, but they should be hung anyway."

"That was your father and mine riding up there," Nathan announced. "I should signal them."

"Couldn't we just ride back to town. I mean, the fewer the people who know, the better."

Nathan scowled, lifted his rifle into the air, and fired off two rapid shots. In a matter of moments he saw the dust of two riders coming toward them out of the cottonwood grove.

"I'm glad you're safe, Colin. I was really worried about you being hurt or something. The Lord really answered my prayers."

"Well, next time pray that I'll still have my clothes on!"

"Next time? Do you plan on making a habit of this? What were you doing down here anyway, instead of staying up in the trees?"

"I was hoping to sneak along the sage toward town and then to go home after dark."

"Why didn't you signal me sooner?"

"I was back over against those hills, and I couldn't tell who was with you. From that distance, I could spot Onepenny, so I knew it was you. But I wasn't sure of the other two. I had to come closer and make sure Leah wasn't with you."

"Leah? Yeah, that could have been real interesting!" Nathan laughed.

"Riggins, if you ever, ever tell anyone in Galena about this, you will suffer a slow and tortuous death, I promise you!"

Colin was mounted on Onepenny behind Nathan when they met their fathers on the trail. After a few minutes of explanation, they turned their horses back toward Galena.

"Marshal, you have to catch them and see that they are hung," Colin insisted.

"Well, son, the punishment I'll leave to a judge and jury, but I will try to trace them down. I'm not about to ride up in those mountains after dark, but I'll get a couple of men together in the morning, and we'll pick up the trail. I'll wire up north too. They sound like the type bound to show up at a saloon sooner or later."

No one talked much on the return trip. It was after sundown when they rode down the rutted, dusty Main Street. The ever-pounding presence of the Shiloh stamp mills echoed in the distance. There were no shouts from the saloons, no shots in the street, no freight wagons creaking—not even a barking dog.

It was exceedingly calm.

But no one seemed to notice.

Nathan rode Onepenny out to Shipley's to check on Thunder. Tona crouched at the buffalo's gate as if it were his assignment in life to watch the beast.

"Well, Tona, he looks fed, settled, and asleep on the hoof. You really don't have to sit here all night."

Tona tilted his head and whacked his tail in the dirt. But he didn't budge, even when Nathan rode back to town. Nathan put Onepenny away for the night in the corral next to the livery and walked toward home.

Lights flickered out of the shops and houses.

Nathan heard the sound of his boot heels slapping the wooden sidewalk.

Then the sound of a shot came from across town.

He heard a man's shout.

A woman's high-pitched laughter.

And a curse.

A crowd flooded into the street, then ebbed back into the Cimarron Club.

Just a typical Galena Saturday night!

6

On every Saturday at 5:01 P.M., 284 mostly single male employees of the Shiloh mine got paid, as did those who worked for the Ratchet, the Elmira, and the Double Donkey. By 5:30 P.M. cowboys from the 707, the McGuire, the Pronghorn, the Running R, and the Circle XL ranches would hit town with a galloping thunder. And by 6:00 P.M. citizens could count on the first report of fights.

Despite all this confusion, Sunday mornings were usually calm at the Riggins home. Nathan's mom busied herself in the kitchen with the last details of Sunday dinner. His dad spent Saturday nights sleeping at his office or patrolling the streets.

On this particular Sunday morning, if town was quiet enough, Marshal Riggins and two deputies would ride out to try to locate the traders who had stripped Colin. Church would not start until 10:00 A.M.

Nathan always brought in extra firewood on Saturday nights and was allowed to sleep late on Sunday mornings—not that he was always sleepy. With a cotton flannel sheet pulled up to his neck and only one quilt on his bed, he opened his eyes and stared at the ceiling.

Maybe I could charge a nickel each for any who wanted to come see Thunder. If I got, say, twenty customers per day, that would be a dollar a day! A few handbills around town, maybe a big sign over by the stage stop—Nathan T. Riggins Presents Thunder—Nevada's Last Buffalo.

"Thunder!" Nathan groaned as he sat straight up in bed. "I've got a buffalo to feed!"

"Nathan," a voice shouted, "haul out here as quick as you can!"

"Dad?" Nathan hopped across the floor pulling on his britches. "Dad? I thought you went out looking for—"

"A busy night. But I'll be riding out soon. You get dressed and go get that buffalo of yours."

"Thunder?"

"Yeah, he just ate the mayor's entire garden and has chased about every horse on Main Street."

"How'd he get loose? What's he doing out? Where is he?" Nathan pulled on his boots.

"I don't know how he got loose, but he's only a few minutes away from being Sunday dinner," his father reported. "I'm leaving to track down Colin's abductors, so you'll have to round him up by yourself."

"Nathan," his mother called, "don't be late for church!"

Running out into the street, Nathan heard dogs barking furiously over on the west side of town. He sprinted most of the way and found Tona and a small pack of dogs penning Thunder against a remnant of a wooden fence behind Mrs. Gregory's house.

"Tona, what happened? How did Thunder get here?"

The dog didn't answer.

Nathan's sudden presence gave the dogs added confidence. They stalked toward the buffalo, who spun around and ran right through the fence, scattering boards everywhere. Then he cut down an alley and routed out two cowboys sleeping on the bench in front of Big Leonard's. He trotted past the row of privies toward the hills behind town. Nathan turned and ran straight for the livery.

Tossing his saddle on Onepenny, he quickly climbed aboard and raced after the buffalo. Tona met them by the back of the burn pile.

Nathan had only come within a hundred feet or so when the buffalo ran straight at him. Nathan cut Onepenny to the right and avoided the charge. But Thunder turned and rushed them again.

"Man, no matter where we turn, he's coming right at us! Hey, that's it! He can just chase us back to the corral."

Nathan zigzagged Onepenny right and left all the way back to the edge of town and Shipley's corral. Thunder ran after them—sometimes charging, sometimes trotting, sometimes walking. When they reached the corral, Nathan saw that the gate stood open.

"Somebody let him out! Someone had to open that gate, Onepenny!"

To Nathan's great surprise Thunder trotted right into the corral and over to the water trough, which was almost dry. Nathan slid down off Onepenny and quickly closed the gate.

On the way back to the house, he spotted Mr. Mercee loading something out of his blacksmith shop. Within a few minutes, Nathan had a piece of chain dragging in the dirt behind him. He swung into his yard, dropped the chain, and raced into the house. He emerged a few minutes later with a key lock in one hand and a piece of toast in the other. He crammed the toast into his mouth as he raced back to Shipley's corral dragging the chain. With the corral gate secured and locked, he stowed the key in his pocket and rode Onepenny home.

Nathan scrubbed his face and neck, changed his clothes,

cleaned his fingernails, and was ready to walk to church when his mother emerged from the bedroom.

"I trust you took care of that buffalo business?"

"Yes, ma'am. He's in the corral, and the gate is chain-locked. He won't be eating up anyone else's garden."

■

Nathan was surprised to see Leah sitting with her stepmother in church. Sliding in next to her, he whispered, "What are you doing home already?"

"Doc Stanton was out all night and rode back by this morning, so I just rode in with him."

"Are Mrs. Dodge and the baby . . . you know, okay?"

"Yep. She was up cookin' breakfast," Leah murmured as the worship service began.

After church Nathan told Leah about the morning's dash to recover Thunder.

"He's rather a bother, ain't he?" she commented.

"Actually, if folks would just leave him alone, he'd not—"

"But that's the bother in it. Folks ain't goin' to leave him alone. They ain't never had a buffalo in Nevada before."

"I don't expect any more trouble," Nathan mumbled. "Did you hear what happened to Colin?"

"I saw he wasn't in church."

"Some outlaws stole his horse and saddle and stuff, but he wasn't hurt."

"When?" she gasped.

"Yesterday . . . on the way home. While I was out there at the Dodge place looking for you."

"Stuff? What do you mean they stole his stuff?" she asked.

Nathan shrugged. "You know . . . his woolly chaps and—"

"They stole those? What on earth for?" She smiled.

"Beats me, but outlaws aren't always known for being smart," Nathan replied.

"What else did they steal?"

Nathan started to walk on toward home. "What do you mean, what else?"

"You know. Did they take his boots?"

"Yep."

"His . . . eh, shirt?"

"Yep."

"His—"

Nathan interrupted, "Look, if you want to know what they stole, you just march up there to his big house on the hill and ask him yourself!"

"Well, you don't have to get uppity!"

"The important thing is that Colin's not hurt, and he's back home," Nathan explained.

"Did your daddy go riding after those men?"

"Yeah, but he can't chase them any further than the county line."

"Nathan, after dinner could you and me practice sayin' our lines? Miss D'Imperio wants me to have them all memorized by this Wednesday, and I need some help."

"Yeah. I'll meet you over at Shipley's," he suggested.

"Why Shipley's?"

"'Cause there's nobody there but Tona and a buffalo," he answered.

"Thanks, Nathan. And remember," she giggled, "if I perish, I perish!"

■

When Nathan finished eating a dinner of fried chicken, boiled rice, canned stewed tomatoes, baked acorn squash, and warm bread pudding with raisins and brown sugar, he asked to be excused. Miss D'Imperio, who rotated her meals among the parents of Galena, had eaten with them. She and Nathan's mother were discussing quilt patterns when he cleared his dishes off the table, left the house, and walked toward Shipley's.

Leah joined him in front of the Mercantile.

"I saw Colin's mother, and she said his feet were so sore he couldn't put on his boots. That's why he didn't come to church," Leah reported. "I used to walk barefoot all the time. It ain't so bad."

"Well, Colin probably isn't used to it."

"Did you tell Miss D'Imperio what we were doing?" she asked.

"Yep."

"What did she say?"

"She said she had found the perfect material for your costume and was going to work on it tomorrow night."

"Really? She said that?" Leah beamed.

Nathan turned quickly to stare Leah in the eyes, and then suddenly he blurted out, "'Don't think that you can escape in the king's house, any more than all the other Jews. For if you don't speak out, then someone else will deliver the Jews, but you and your family will be destroyed. Who knows, but perhaps you have come to the kingdom for such a time as this?'"

Leah's smile faded, and she replied with arms waving, "'Go, gather together all the Jews in Shushan, and fast for me, and neither eat nor drink three days, night or day. My maidens and I will fast too, and then I will go to the king . . . to the king . . . the king, WHICH is not permitted by the law; and if I perish, I perish!'"

Suddenly she hugged Nathan and danced around in a circle shouting, "I did it, Nathan. I did it and you didn't have to help me at all!"

Realizing what she was doing, Leah pulled her hands away from Nathan and blushed. They continued walking, neither speaking for a moment.

"Nathan? Did you ever wish you had a brother or sister?"

"Yeah, sometimes."

"You and me—we're kind of like a brother and sister . . . ain't we?"

"I suppose so."

"Ya know, we ain't knowed each other for a year, but it seems like it's been a long, long time, don't it?" Leah nodded.

"Yep."

"Nathan, I got a question for you. Now I know that Queen Esther needed to break one of the laws of Shushan to try to save her people, but didn't she know that the Lord would save her? I mean, if she really trusted the Almighty, she wouldn't have to worry about perishing, right?"

"I don't know, but it seems to me," Nathan shrugged, "that people ought to do what God wants them to do—no matter what. I don't think He always guarantees we'll have a happy ending."

"You mean, she could have obeyed God and got killed anyway?"

"I think maybe that's a question for Reverend Clarenton."

"Yeah . . . but . . . you mean she was really afraid? I thought maybe those lines was just melodramatic. You think she really was scared of dying?"

"Why not?"

"It makes my lines kind of scary, don't it?" she said, eyes wide.

Suddenly, Nathan began to run. "What's that? What's happening at Shipley's?"

Wagons, horses, and people crowded around the corral. Nathan raced toward the barn with Leah a few steps behind. Tona ran out to greet him. As he approached, he noticed the repaired wagon of Hawthorne H. Miller. The photographer had set up his camera and was taking pictures of people posed in front of the corral by the captured buffalo.

"What's going on here?" Nathan shouted.

From under the black canvas at the back of the camera Miller shouted, "Get out of the picture, son. You'll have to wait your turn!"

Nathan jumped back, and the powder flashed as a picture was taken. Thunder paced back and forth, irritated by the confusion outside the corral.

"Now, son, if you'll just—"

"Mr. Miller, what are you doing with my buffalo, and how did that top rail come off the corral?"

"The Riggins lad. My word, of course I'll take your picture. After all, he is your buffalo! Just wait in line behind these other fine people." Then he turned to the crowd gathered there. "That's right, folks, you can have a photograph of your whole family with the legendary buffalo, Thunder. Why, you can send this to the relatives back East. What sport it will be! Yes, just line up behind the little blonde girl here and have your cash dollar ready!"

"Mr. Miller," Nathan insisted, "you can't pester my buffalo like this! If he gets mad, he could sail right over the top of this short rail!"

"Nonsense. You have him chained in there quite nicely, may I add. And you did give me exclusive rights to photograph him in the corral, didn't you? You are a lad of your word, I presume?"

"I said you could take a picture, but not set up a circus!"

"Son, you're slowing things down. You run along. I do have a present for you."

Miller reached into the back of his wagon and removed a photograph and handed it to Nathan. "Came out rather well, wouldn't you say? That's your copy."

Nathan stared at the large picture of Thunder charging Miller's camera.

"Let me see, Nathan!" Leah tugged at the photograph.

He handed it to her. "That is a really great picture, Mr. Miller."

"Fine. Now you two run along. I promise I'll replace the rail as soon I accommodate these outstanding citizens. And if anything's open in town, go buy you and your very attractive girlfriend a sweet!" He handed Nathan a quarter.

"Actually, she's not my—"

Suddenly, Leah grabbed him by the arm and kicked him hard in the shin.

"What did you do that for?"

"You were about to say something stupid." She wrinkled her nose and the freckles danced. "I saw Mr. Welenky open his store for the foreman of the Circle XL. Maybe we can catch him and buy a licorice."

"Mr. Miller," Nathan called, "this is the last day for taking pictures."

"Thank you, son. I will see that you get the rest of your royalties."

"Royalties?"

"Yes, Hawthorne H. Miller is a professional. I don't expect to make money off your animal without you getting a profit. Say about five cents for every photograph sold?"

"Five cents?" Nathan coughed.

"He wouldn't consider it for less than a dime!" Leah put in with a fake scowl.

"Actually, I didn't think—"

"Now, Nathan, don't be greedy," Leah interrupted. "Ten cents will be just fine."

"My word," Miller fumed, "I should say so. Yes, yes, a dime it will be. Now go on . . . go on."

Leah pulled Nathan back away from the crowd and toward town.

"You ain't no good at all at bargainin'," she teased.

"A dime for doing nothing? That doesn't seem fair."

"Well, I sure do hope you marry a money-smart girl 'cause you're going to need help, Nathan Riggins!"

■

Sunday evening seemed too quiet to Nathan. His mother was reading *Moby Dick*, trying to find the symbolism that Miss D'Imperio had suggested it contained. His father was still out on the trail. The streets were hushed because the miners and cowboys were either broke or sleeping it off—or both.

He had no school assignments left, no book he wanted to read, no game to play, no chores to do. He took a piece of left-over chicken from the hamper and ate it standing in the open front door watching the evening sunset. The sky was blue as a robin's egg, but the blue was fading, and the breeze felt cool, as if you were fanning yourself with a wet rag.

The skin of the chicken was especially crisp and the meat juicy. "Mother, you know . . . sometimes Galena can really be boring!" Nathan returned to the kitchen and wiped his hands on a flowered towel.

"What, dear?"

"I said, there's nothing to do!"

"Yes, that's why I like Sundays so much. Don't you think it's nice to have one day when we aren't so busy?"

"Oh, I guess. Say, can I walk over to Colin's? I want to see how he's doing."

"Yes. Take that basket on the table back to Mrs. Maddison, would you?"

"Yes, ma'am."

Nathan cut across the street, up the alley, and down Main Street where he picked up Tona. After several raps on the door, Colin appeared, peeking out a crack in the curtains. He flung open the door.

"Nathan," Colin groaned, "what do you want?"

"Hi, Colin. Hey, this is for your mother. And I was just wondering how you were doing. I mean, I haven't seen you all day."

"Well, I've spent the day demanding that we move to another state."

"What?"

"At a minimum I'm dropping out of school."

"You're what?" Nathan gasped.

"Don't you see? I can't walk through town ever again. Everybody knows. Everyone will laugh!"

Nathan relaxed and shifted his weight from one foot to the other. "You didn't have any choice about giving your stuff to those outlaws. It could have happened to anyone."

"But it didn't happen to anyone. It happened to me!"

"Colin, no one in town knows but your dad, my dad, and me."

"You told Leah, didn't you?" Colin accused.

"I told her about you losing your horse and stuff, but I sure didn't mention you needing my blanket."

"You really didn't tell Leah everything?"

"Nope."

"Honest to God?"

"I don't lie, Colin."

"You promise that you will never ever tell another living soul in this town—cross your heart and hope to die?"

"I promise."

"Well," Colin said sighing, "I guess I could try one more day of school just to see how it goes."

"Great! We couldn't get along without you. You make a great Haman!"

"Oh . . . the play! If I'm going back to school, I've got to learn my lines! Bye, Nathan!"

Suddenly, the door slammed with Nathan still staring at the curtained glass. He turned slowly. As he walked across the street, he saw Mr. Mercee, the blacksmith.

"Nathan, did that piece of chain work for the buffalo?"

"Yes, sir. Thank you. Say, Mr. Mercee, I was wondering. How would a person build a corral guaranteed to be buffalo-stout? I mean, I know Thunder can bust out of a railroad car, and he ran right through an old cabin."

"I saw a corral built using railroad rails for posts and one-inch-thick flat-iron bolted on for cross pieces," Mr. Mercee reported. "I don't think a train could have steamed out of that pen."

"Wouldn't that cost a lot of money?" Nathan asked.

"It sure would if you used new material. But a place like the Shiloh or one of the other mines has lots of scrap iron around. Maybe a fellow could make a deal with them. You fixin' on upgrading the corral?"

"I don't know," Nathan responded. "It's just that Thunder attracts so many people. I'd feel safer if he were more secure."

"Well, son . . . if you ever need my help with such a project, let me know. I think having a resident buffalo might be good for Galena."

"Yes, sir."

"Anyway, Nate, don't worry. I saw the corral this afternoon. It looks plenty stout to me."

Nathan had just left Mr. Mercee when a cowboy ran up the ally and pulled a Henry repeating rifle out of the scabbard on a blood-bay horse standing at the rail.

"What's going on?" Nathan shouted.

"There's a buffalo going wild out behind the Cimarron Club. He just leveled the outhouse, and he headed for the water tank!"

"What are you going to do with that Henry?" Nathan hollered.

"Shoot him, of course," the man yelled as he ran back up the alley.

7

Nathan sprinted past the cowboy with the rifle and reached the back of the Cimarron Club. He couldn't believe his eyes. Before a gleeful watching crowd, Hawthorne H. Miller was trying to subdue Thunder with a cane in one hand and an open umbrella in the other.

Seeing Mr. Norco, owner of the Cimarron, Nathan shouted, "Don't let them shoot my buffalo!"

Ned Norco, who could lift two men off the ground at a time, grabbed the pursuing cowboy by the neck and relieved him of his rifle.

"Don't mind Rawley. He's just sore 'cause he was in the outhouse at the time!" the big man shouted.

Seeing Nathan, Miller stopped chasing the buffalo to catch his breath.

"Riggins! Thank heavens, you're here. My word, get that brute back in the corral, would you? At least back into what's left of the corral."

"What's left of it? What happened?"

Leah ran up to Nathan.

"Well, this . . . this monster, this buffalo of yours tried to jump right over the corral!" Miller huffed.

"Leah," Nathan ordered, "go saddle Onepenny and bring him here! I'm afraid one of these men will shoot Thunder if I leave." Then turning back to Miller, he probed, "So

79

Thunder jumped out? I told you it was dangerous to take down that top—"

"No, he didn't jump out!" Miller interrupted. "I said he tried to jump out. Actually, he hit the rails and sort of . . . you know . . . busted his way through."

"Through the two-by-eights?"

"Like they were matchsticks."

Nathan was relieved to see his father ride up and send the crowd back into the Cimarron Club. Then the marshal came over to Nathan and Miller. The buffalo stood silently staring at them from fifty feet away.

"You spent all day, and you haven't got him penned yet?" the marshal asked.

"I corralled him this morning, but he busted out again this evening," Nathan explained.

"Marshal, it's my fault actually. I'm afraid I underestimated the animal's ferocity."

"And who are you?"

"Hawthorne H. Miller, photographer, lecturer, and author. No doubt you've read about me."

"I've never heard of you." The marshal shrugged. "But if you're responsible for that buffalo escaping, then you're responsible for rebuilding the Cimarron Club outhouse. Is that clear?"

"Yes, sir." Miller nodded. "Say, it would be a splendid photograph to have father and son posed next to the Galena mascot. I could run get my wagon and—"

The glare from Marshal Riggins's eyes silenced Miller.

Nathan's father reached into his black leather vest and pulled out his pocket watch. "Nathan, I've got to send a couple wires out. Get this animal back into the corral, and do it immediately."

"Yes, sir." Nathan glanced at his father sitting, as always, straight up in the saddle. "Ah . . . did you find those men who stole Colin's belongings?"

"Nope. We tracked them to the county line, but I don't have any jurisdiction further than that. That's why I need to wire up to Elko County. Chances are, they will be trying to peddle things there tonight."

The marshal rode back toward the center of town, tipping his hat to Leah as she rode up on Onepenny. Hawthorne Miller retreated to the Cimarron Club, leaving Nathan, Leah, Onepenny, Tona, and several other barking dogs to confront the buffalo. Nathan climbed up into the saddle, and Leah slipped on behind him.

"What do we do now?" she asked.

"Well . . . I think this will work!" He spurred Onepenny toward the buffalo and then veered him off at the last minute. Once again Thunder started chasing after them. Within a few minutes he had led the buffalo back to the Shipley place. With Leah still mounted, Nathan dropped down and unlocked the gate.

"He'll just come through those busted boards again," she warned.

"Not until he's through eating," Nathan replied. He grabbed a couple arm loads of hay from the barn and scattered them on the side of the corral furthest from the broken rails.

He had just exited and remounted Onepenny when the buffalo trotted back into the pen. Again Nathan jumped down and locked the gate.

"Leah, I need to talk to Mr. Mercee. I think maybe he can put an iron rail or two over here and keep Thunder penned. But I need you to sit on Onepenny right in front of this break until I come back. I don't think he'll try anything with you two blocking the path."

"What if he tries to escape?"

"Then get out of his way because you couldn't stop him if you wanted to."

■

It was almost dark when Mr. Mercee finished bolting two flat-iron top rails to the Shipley corral.

"There you go, son. They'll hold him for a while. Once he really tries though, he'll snap those posts off at the dirt line."

"Thanks, Mr. Mercee! I'll try to figure a better setup."

He rode back to the livery and left Onepenny and then walked Leah to her house. When he reached his own house, his mother and father were sitting at the kitchen table. From the serious expression on their faces, he knew they'd been talking about him.

It was his father who spoke. "Nate . . . this buffalo thing. It's just not working."

"Dad, this is just the first day. I'm sure—"

"Nathan," his mother broke in, "we just don't have a secure enough place. Wouldn't it be better for him to run out on the prairie?"

"Mother, he'd be shot in a week."

"Son, animals don't live forever. Besides he lasted all winter."

"But he didn't choose to be out here! It's not fair. There must be a way to keep him safe!" Nathan insisted.

"Well," his mother added, "if we had a zoo or something, then everyone could enjoy watching him."

"A zoo! Yeah, Galena could build a zoo and—"

"Nathan, Galena isn't large enough for a zoo. Maybe Virginia City or Sacramento."

"No, not California. He's the only buffalo in Nevada.

How about Carson City? Don't you think the state capital should have a buffalo?" Nathan suggested.

"Well, that does make a lot more sense than keeping him here in Galena," his father agreed.

"You could write to the governor and tell him you'd like to donate a buffalo for the cultural heritage of the people of Nevada," his mother suggested.

"Wh-what?" Nathan stammered.

Mrs. Riggins laughed. "I'll help you write the letter."

■

Actually, it turned out to be Miss D'Imperio and his friends who wrote most of it. When Nathan told her about it the next day at school, she decided it would be a good lesson in grammar and government for the older students. They spent three days working on the text and form. By the end of class Wednesday, a carefully printed letter was inserted into an envelope addressed to "The Honorable John H. Kinkead, Governor of the State of Nevada, State Capital, Carson City, Nevada."

Nathan walked home from school, which met in the back room of the Welsh Miners' Hall, with Leah and Colin.

"You going to take that letter to the post office?" Leah asked.

"Nope. They don't send the mail out until the morning stage. I'm going down to the Overland office and see that this gets on the evening stage to Battle Mountain Station. They'll put it on the train there, and it could be in Carson City by tomorrow."

"Well, I'm going to the post office," Leah announced, "because I just might be gettin' some mail!"

"You really didn't tell her, did you?" Colin whispered as Leah crossed the street.

"Nope."

"Well, I think maybe we won't be leaving Galena after all."

"Great! This calls for a celebration. I'll race you to the Mercantile. Loser buys the factory creme fills!"

"Riggins, you cheat. You can't start running! You didn't say one, two, three, go! Riggins!"

The voice was fading behind Nathan as he crashed through the Mercantile door. It was always the same. He always won. Colin always cried foul. And Nathan always bought his own candy.

Both boys were sprawled on the bench in front of the Mercantile debating the merits of dark chocolate lemon creme fills versus light chocolate ones when Leah ran up with a letter in her hand.

"I knew it! I knew it! Look here! I got another letter from Kylie!"

"Kylie who?" Colin asked with a wink at Nathan.

Leah stuck out her tongue. "He says he'll be comin' to visit after all. His daddy can't come down, but he'll be on the stage from Silver City and should get here Wednesday next."

"When did he write the letter?" Colin asked.

"Eh . . . Saturday. Why?"

"Then that means he's coming in today," Colin informed her.

"Today! No, not today! I'm not ready. I'm not . . . today? Are you sure?"

"Today is Wednesday." Nathan nodded. "Doesn't this Kylie have to go to school?"

"He's smart enough without school," Leah bragged. "Nathan, you've got to go to the stage office and wait for him!"

"Oh, no, I already spent one afternoon looking like a fool," he protested.

"Please, Nathan, please? I have to go put on my new brown dress, comb my hair, wash my face, and . . . Please, Nathan, just wait until I get there. I promise I'll hurry! Didn't you say you wanted to get that letter on the stage? Well, just keep an eye out for Kylie, that's all. Please, please, Nathan?"

Nathan sighed and shook his head. "Okay, but this is the last time I do this. Understand?"

"Thanks, Nathan!" Leah hugged him around the neck and then took off running toward home.

"Nathan," Colin began, "do you understand girls?"

"Nope."

"Good."

"Why?"

"'Cause neither do I, and I was afraid maybe I was all alone. Are you going over to the stage now?"

"What time is it?"

Colin pulled out a pocket watch. "Almost 3:30."

"Well, the stage doesn't come in for forty-five minutes. I think I'll check on Onepenny and Thunder first."

"And I'm going to check out mother's pantry," Colin added. "I'll see you at the stage!"

■

Nathan perched in front of the stage office, letter in hand, at 4:00 P.M. Neither Leah nor Colin had arrived. A well-dressed man with shining black boots and a straight-handled cane sat down next to him.

"You waiting to ride the stage, son?"

"No, sir, I've just got an important letter to send out."

The man turned and smiled. "You writing to some cute little girl?"

"No, sir, I'm writing to the governor . . . see?" He held up the envelope. "It was kind of a class project."

"Yes, well that's very good of you. I'm sure John will be pleased to hear from you."

"John? Do you know Governor Kinkead?"

"Yes, indeed. We have dinner together about every Monday evening."

"Are you somebody important—like a judge or something?" Nathan asked.

The man laughed. "Oh, no, I'm not very important at all. My name's Pennington. I happen to own a railroad."

"You own the railroad?" Nathan gasped.

"I'm afraid so, but it's not that important a position. Especially when times are tough. Say, I will be seeing the governor this Saturday. Would you like me to hand-deliver it?"

"Yes, sir! Thank you!" Nathan handed the man the letter. "Say, I was wondering . . . how much would it cost to ship a big animal from Battle Mountain Station to Carson City?"

"How big an animal?"

"Say, a buffalo."

"A buffalo? A buffalo! You have a buffalo?"

"Yes, sir, I bought it from Dakota Williams."

"That buffalo? You have Thunder?"

"Yes, sir." Nathan smiled.

"Son, I wouldn't let that animal within two miles of my rail car! Do you have any idea of the damage he did to our train?"

"He busted out of a freight car."

"He ripped up two freight cars and then charged the engine. He broke so many steam pipes and fittings that the engine was inoperable. No, no, I'm afraid railroad rules state that absolutely no buffaloes can be shipped alive."

"Maybe there can be exceptions to the rule?" Nathan asked hopefully.

"Not hardly. I made the rules!" the man insisted. "Listen, son, why on earth do you want to ship a live buffalo anyway?"

"It's in the letter. Since Thunder is the only buffalo in Nevada, I thought he ought to be in a zoo or something in Carson City."

Mr. Pennington sat up straight on the edge of the bench and leaned both glove-covered hands on the cane.

"Son, that's an excellent idea! Why, if the governor doesn't want him, I'll build a pen at the railroad office . . . yes, yes, something for the easterners. My, won't that be something! Indeed, it's a splendid idea, simply splendid!"

"Then you'll ship him on the railroad after all?" Nathan pushed.

"Oh my heavens, no! You'll have to deliver him of course."

"Deliver him?"

"Yes, yes, you know, like driving cattle or something."

"Mister, if he was calm enough to drive like a cow, he wouldn't have jumped through your freight car."

"I suppose you're right. But still it is a good idea. Perhaps a freight wagon? A stout one of course. Look, here comes the stage!"

"You'll take the letter to the governor?"

"Yes, indeed, and I'm serious about wanting that buffalo in Carson City."

Several people climbed off the stage and unloaded their luggage.

"Now remember," Mr. Pennington continued, "you be

figuring out how to get him to Ormsby County, and I'll take care of the rest."

"Yes, sir. Thank you, sir."

Nathan stood watching the stage, now teamed with six fresh horses, roll out of town. Two men, a woman, and a boy were carrying baggage down the wooden sidewalk when he remembered. *Kylie! I forgot to look for Kylie Collins! Leah will kill me!*

He raced after the departing stage passengers. "Kylie! Kylie!" he screamed.

Suddenly, a tall, broad-shouldered man with shaggy blond hair spun on his spur-jingling boot heels and drew his revolver, pointing it right at Nathan! Nathan's hands shot straight up. "Don't shoot, Mister. I'm not packing a gun!"

The man looked up and down the sidewalk. "Who shouted at me?"

"You're Kylie?" Nathan gasped. The man looked about six feet tall and about twenty-five to thirty years old.

"You yelled at me?" The man's grim expression relaxed, and he reset the hammer of his revolver and jammed it back into his holster.

"Eh . . . yes, sir, I was sent here to meet you."

"Who knew that I was coming?"

"Leah."

"Who?"

"Leah Walker. You wrote her a letter, and she's been expecting you."

"I don't think I know any Leah Walker. What's she look like?"

"You know . . . kind of long brown hair and some freckles . . . and about as tall as me . . . a real pretty smile and—"

"How old is this Leah?"

"Twelve. But almost thirteen."

"What? Son, you've got the wrong Kylie."

"You're not Kylie Collins?"

"Nah, I'm Kylie Rowtane. Most call me Kid Rowtane."

"Kid Rowtane? Like in the Gold Hill shootout?"

"That's me."

"Kid Rowtane pulled a gun on me—and I lived?" Nathan stammered.

"It's your lucky day. Next time be more careful who you run up to from behind."

"Yes, sir. I will," Nathan stammered. "Ah . . . Mr. Rowtane, was there a Kylie Collins on the stage?"

"Nope."

Rowtane turned and walked on down to the hotel.

"Who was that?"

Nathan whipped around to see Leah in her brown Sunday dress standing behind him.

"Eh . . . that was Kid Rowtane."

"The gunfighter? You know him?"

"Yep."

"What was you talking to him about?"

"Kylie."

"Kylie wasn't on the stage, was he?"

"Nope. But Kid Rowtane was, so I, eh, asked him if he had seen a Kylie."

"And what did he say?"

"Nope."

"I knew it. Wednesday next is next Wednesday. Not today. You'll just have to wait for him next week!"

"Oh, no, not me," Nathan groaned. "But, listen, I did meet Mr. Pennington—you know, the one who owns the railroad? He said he would make sure they'd have a place for Thunder in Carson City if . . ." Nathan's voice trailed off.

"If what?"

"If I'll deliver him to Ormsby County."

"Deliver him? You mean like ship him on a train?"

"I mean, like pack him across the state. The train won't ship buffaloes—especially Thunder."

"Pack him?"

"Yeah, in a wagon."

"You can't keep him in a stout pen. How are you going to haul him in a wagon?"

Nathan walked along the sidewalk and waited for several rigs to pass before he crossed the street. "Mr. Mercee said he could build a buffalo-stout corral if he had the material. Maybe he could build a buffalo-stout wagon."

"Well, I'm going to go change my dress," Leah informed him.

"Why? It looks very nice."

"Of course it looks nice. That's why I'm saving it for Kylie!" she huffed.

■

As Nathan explained the situation, Mr. Mercee's eyes gleamed with the challenge. Soon he was sketching out a design on the back of a used piece of brown paper.

"It will work!" he exclaimed. "It will work! Of course you'll need iron wheels, lots of axle grease, and maybe four mules to pull it, but it will work, Nathan. Providing it doesn't rain and you don't hit sand."

"Yeah, but what will a wagon like that cost?" Nathan asked.

"Well . . . let's see. For such a patriotic cause I'll donate my labor; and for supplies, if we buy some of the things used, why, it can be built for two hundred dollars."

"Two hundred dollars? Two hundred dollars!" Nathan

moaned. "Where in the world will I come up with two hundred dollars?"

"Well, if you do, I'd be honored to build such a wagon. 'Mercee's Buffalo-Tight' we'll call it. I might get orders for others. Of course they'd cost more," he mumbled, "much more."

Nathan walked toward his house without glancing at anyone around him.

Lord, I should have never brought him in. I should have let Thunder wander out there on the plains until he ended up as a robe around some Indian lady or supper for some cowboys. Two hundred dollars! Lord, it would take me five summers to earn that much.

He didn't notice the men in a heated discussion in front of the Cimarron Club until one of them grabbed his shoulder. Nathan glanced up to see Hawthorne H. Miller.

"Riggins, my boy—just the lad I need to talk to. The boys and I have been talking, and I've got a splendid idea. How would you and your buffalo like to make two, three, maybe even five hundred dollars?"

8

*F*ive hundred dollars!" Nathan choked. "You've got a way I can legally make five hundred dollars?"

"Well, at least two hundred, but perhaps more," Miller blustered, throwing his arm around Nathan's shoulder.

"Now here's the situation." Nathan squirmed out from under the man's arm. "Perhaps we should find a private place to talk," Miller suggested.

"How about my dad's office?"

"The marshal? Ah, yes . . . of course."

They crossed the street and walked to the jail. Deputy Hailey sat behind the desk.

"Nathan, your dad headed home after sending those wires. Who's this guy?"

"I am Hawthorne H. Miller—respected writer, photographer, and—"

"Well, I ain't never heard of you."

"Mr. Hailey, this man has a deal for me. How about you listening to it?" Nathan requested.

Nathan and Miller sat down in chairs across from the deputy.

"Now here's the arrangement," Miller explained. "The boys from Rocking R just drove up 2,000 head of cattle from Mexico for the army to feed the Indians at Fort McDermitt.

But while they were in Mexico, several got in a high-stakes poker game. Well, they ended up winning a prize fighting bull."

"You mean the type that's trained for the bullfights?" the deputy asked.

"Exactly. And they drove it up here with the rest of the animals."

"What are they going to do with it? Bullfights are illegal in the states," Nathan questioned.

"Now just wait, I'll get to it. Anyway, the boys say this is the meanest bull they ever been around. He'll charge every one and everything in the corral. He's hooked half the boys at the Running R. They've been trying to figure what to do with him, and we came to a solution. Here's the deal. We build a big corral, set up some bleachers, and then sell tickets."

"Tickets to what?"

"To the bull versus the buffalo."

"What?"

"The two animals will be put into the arena to fight it out. Winner takes all—so to speak."

"That's crazy!" Nathan exclaimed.

"It would draw a crowd," Deputy Hailey conceded.

"That it will. And we can make handbills and distribute them all over the county. We'll charge one dollar. It will be a real money-maker. And your part will be guaranteed. No matter how well your buffalo does or doesn't do, you get the same amount. I'll put it all together. All you have to do is show up and supply the buffalo. What do you say, son?"

"I say it sounds crazy!"

"Are you turning me down?"

"Not necessarily. I just said it sounds crazy. I don't want to hurt the buffalo."

"Well, what's it going to be? I need to know."

"I'll have to think on it awhile, Mr. Miller."

"You what?"

"Miller," Deputy Hailey interjected, "he said he'll think about it. I'll walk you to your hotel room. Need to make my rounds anyway. You go on home, Nate. Talk it over with your folks."

"Splendid!" Miller mused. "We'll stop by the Cimarron for a nightcap. I'm buying."

"You are going to your room," Hailey stated bluntly.

Hawthorne H. Miller was still mumbling protests when Nathan hurried up the now-darkening street toward his house. He spent almost two hours talking about the offer to his mom and dad, and as he crawled into bed, he still hadn't decided what to do.

"Nate?"

"Yeah, Dad."

"Your mother and I will support your decision. But he's your buffalo. It's your call."

"Yes, sir. I know."

"Maybe you better spend some time talking to the Lord about it."

"Yes, sir."

His dad blew out the lantern, and Nathan stared at the darkness.

Lord . . . it's me. This whole thing is crazy. I mean, I want to do what's best for Thunder. Now I think he would live longer and be more protected if he was in Carson City, but I can't get him there without this money from facing a bull. If I don't do something pretty soon, Dad is right. He'll break out of Shipley's and someone will shoot him.

And if he gets hurt or killed by that bull, it will be all wasted effort. Lord, I wish I knew who would win the fight. Then I'd know what to do.

Nathan's mind drifted to the buffalo . . . to Onepenny . . . then to Leah. Suddenly his lines in the play came to mind, and he instinctively mumbled, "'And who knows whether you have come to the kingdom for such a time as this?'"

Suddenly he sat straight up in bed.

"Lord, if I'm going to make a mistake, I'm going to make it trying to do what I think is right—not by doing nothing at all!"

Hawthorne H. Miller holed up in his hotel room all the next day. Nathan was anxious to talk to him, but he was not taking any visitors. It was after school about 4:30 P.M. when a telegram was brought to Nathan's front door.

"Is it for me? Is it from the governor?"

"No." His mother frowned at him. "It's for your father —from the sheriff up in Elko County. Dad must be around town somewhere. Please, go find him. It might be important."

Nathan found his dad helping the Jorgensens reset the wheel on their wagon.

"Dad, you got a wire from Elko County. Maybe it's about Colin's horse!"

"My hands are greasy. Read it to me."

Marshal Riggins, Galena
   Two men answering your descriptions were incarcerated here on Sunday night for drunk and disorderly conduct. They were released Monday

morning and told to promptly exit the city, which they did. They go by the names Hollis Gray and Lorenzo Mourning. Gray is sporting a pair of woolly chaps.

Sheriff Dan Peters, Elko County.

"Drifters . . . probably won't see them in this area again," his dad commented. "How about you taking that wire to Mr. Maddison?"

■

On Thursday Nathan reported to Miss D'Imperio and the class about talking to Mr. Pennington and about the bull/buffalo fight suggested by Mr. Miller. On Friday the whole class discussed a plan, and by the time Nathan, Leah, and Colin met with Mr. Miller, Nathan was ready.

"Well, son," Hawthorne Miller questioned, "what are these other youngsters doing here? Isn't Thunder your buffalo?"

"Yes, sir, but we decided to make a class project out of this."

"Class project? What do you mean?"

"Well, it's sort of a class project to get the buffalo to Carson City, and we see this as a school fund-raiser."

"Yes, yes, of course . . . that will look good on the hand-bill! Then you have agreed to stage the contest?"

"Not until our terms are met."

"Your terms?"

"Yes," Leah answered. "We have a list of requirements."

"A list?" Miller gulped.

Nathan nodded and informed him, "Yes, I will agree if:

1. *The school will be given a minimum guarantee of two hundred dollars.*
2. *The exact purse will be split with 40 percent going to the Rocking R, 40 percent to the class project, and 20 percent to Mr. Hawthorne H. Miller."*

"A mere 20 percent?" he huffed.
Nathan hardly looked up. "I'm not through.

3. *Mr. Miller will pay for all publicity and printing costs for promoting the event.*
4. *Mr. Miller is the exclusive photographer of the event and will be allowed to sell his services during the show.*
5. *The bull/buffalo match will be preceded by a trick riding act, by two songs from the school Glee Club, and a performance of the play,* The Queen Makes a Stand.*"*

Miller ran his fingers nervously through his graying hair and nodded. "A multi-act show . . . yes, yes, that's good, but—"
"There's more," Nathan continued.

"6. *The contest will be held in the stockyard next to the Lander County Livery, which Mr. Petterson will donate for that purpose in exchange for the exclusive right to board the horses of all folks who ride in for the event.*
7. *The bleachers will be built by the Galena Mercantile and the lumber will belong to them after the event. This they will do for free in exchange for being given the exclusive right to sell refreshments to those watching the performance.*
8. *At any point in the match should the hands for the Running R or Mr. Nathan T. Riggins signal to quit, the animals will be separated, and the other side declared the winner."*

"Well," Mr. Miller puffed, "I can see you have given this quite some consideration. And to tell you the truth, several of your ideas are splendid, simply splendid. However, others are quite impossible. To begin with, the distribution of ticket money I cannot accept—"

"Mr. Miller," Colin announced in a tone born into bankers, "the points of this agreement are not open to negotiation. You can accept them or reject them. We will give you until 5:00 P.M. to answer."

With that, Nathan, Colin, and Leah marched out of the room. They giggled all the way down the sidewalk.

"You did real good, Colin." Leah smiled. "You've done your daddy proud!"

"Time for a creme fill!" Nathan shouted and dashed for the Mercantile.

"Nathan!" Colin called, "Hey, wait up! I'm not buying! Did you hear me?"

At 5:01 P.M. Hawthorne H. Miller signed his yet-to-be-famous signature on an agreement right next to Nathan's and Miss D'Imperio's. After Miller left, she turned to Nathan.

"Congratulations, young man. You did a good job."

"Now all I have to do is keep Thunder penned for two weeks!"

"And practice your lines for the play," she reminded him.

"And practice my trick riding," he added.

On the following Tuesday, Nathan received a letter from the governor accepting Thunder for the state of Nevada and inviting Nathan, Miss D'Imperio, and other representatives of the school to come to Carson City and meet with him when they brought the buffalo.

On Wednesday Galena, Battle Mountain Station, Austin, and most of Lander County were plastered with handbills trumpeting the great bull/buffalo fight and talent show. That day Nathan T. Riggins also waited again at the stage office to welcome the mysterious Kylie Collins.

Collins did not arrive.

On Thursday the Galena Mercantile began to build bleachers that would seat one thousand people next to the stockyards.

On Friday Colin broke out with a rash over most of his body. That same day, convinced by mounting enthusiasm for the great event, Mr. Abel Mercee began to build "Mercee's Buffalo-Tight #1" in front of his blacksmith shop.

The following Monday, a meeting of parents and community leaders decided that, pending a positive outcome from the great event, Miss D'Imperio, Nathan, Colin, and Leah would travel to Carson City with the buffalo and meet the governor personally. Mr. Mercee was the unanimous choice to drive the wagon west, since he was the only man alive who would know how to repair the wagon if necessary. His acceptance speech in front of the Cimarron Club lasted almost thirty minutes and effectively cleared the street.

The Shiloh mine and the other smaller ones all declared the coming event a holiday and planned to shut down so miners could attend. Word spread that mines in other towns had also decided to halt operations for the one day.

The cowhands at the Rocking R soon spread the news to outfits from as far away as Idaho and Wyoming. Marshal Riggins enlisted twelve men to act as special deputies for the coming weekend. And most of the saloons in town ordered extra supplies.

Hawthorne H. Miller, anxious to attract a larger crowd, added several more events to the program—Mexican music, Basque folk dances, an Oregon man and his trained dogs, a Hangtown man doing trick shooting, and a wild horse-breaking contest.

On the Tuesday before the great event, the stage lines announced they would run four extra coaches on Friday and Saturday to bring folks down from the Battle Mountain Station train depot.

As the excitement grew, Colin, Leah, and Nathan grew nervous. On the Wednesday afternoon before the performance, the three sat in the empty bleachers overlooking the freshly whitewashed stockyards.

"Nathan, I couldn't sleep last night. Every time I'd close my eyes I was in front of a thousand people, and I couldn't remember my lines."

"Yeah, it's been worrying me too, Leah. Even if we remember our lines, who could hear us in this big crowd anyway?"

"Maybe we'll be lucky and nobody will show up," Colin suggested as he scratched his rash.

"They have to show up! That's how we'll raise the money for the trip!" Leah huffed. "I ain't never been to Carson City before."

"I almost met the governor once," Colin boasted.

"I don't know why we had to have the play out in the arena. It was supposed to be just for parents and such," she complained.

"Miss D'Imperio said it's a great opportunity to teach a Bible lesson to all the miners and cowboys," Nathan reminded her.

"What lesson?" Colin asked.

"You know—that there are some times a person just has to stand up and do what is right regardless of the consequences," Nathan responded.

"Yeah," Leah blurted, "and that we've all been put on earth for a purpose, and we better stand up when it's our appointed time!"

"Do you really think anyone will hear that message?" Colin replied sarcastically.

"If I don't forget my lines!" Leah replied.

"And if they can hear us," Nathan added. "Come on, let's try it again."

"Oh, boy, we've gone over this two dozen times," Colin groaned. "We all know our lines."

"Come on, Colin." Leah grabbed both boys' arms and led them down the steps.

■

On Friday night Nathan didn't even bother closing his eyes. He stared at the dark ceiling and thought about wild horses, school plays, buffaloes, bulls, Onepenny, iron wagons, Carson City, and a girl with freckles.

Lord, this is real important to all of us, but especially to Leah. Could you help her tomorrow? She doesn't think she can do anything very well . . . and she really wants to impress her father and stepmother. Please, Lord, help Leah and all of us not to mess up.

■

Saturday morning was a blur. People had begun streaming into Galena Friday night, filling up hotels and setting up tents on the west side of town. By the next morning the streets of Galena were clogged with wagons, horses, stages, and pedestrians.

There were rumors of reporters from as far away as San Francisco and St. Joseph. General Miles sent his last minute regrets for canceling his plans to attend. Trouble with the Sioux kept him in the Dakota Territory. And the famous actress and singer, Lynida Tuloski, was rumored to be in town to watch the performance.

Nathan got up before daylight. He and his dad moved Thunder to a pen next to the stockyard. True to form, the buffalo chased Onepenny right into the new corral. Fresh hay and a half-bucket of sweet oats kept him quiet for most of the morning.

The cowboys from the Rocking R ranch herded the bull, which they nicknamed Lightning, into town. The big, sharp-horned brindle bull trailed fine and only turned unruly when anyone or anything entered his corral. During his fourteen hours in Galena the bull had gored two horses, killed one dog outright, and lamed another when it flung the mutt twenty feet into the air.

Mr. Hawthorne H. Miller scurried through the crowds like an overwrought mother. He split his time running from the ticket booths to the barn that served as a backstage room for all the acts. With a large megaphone that he had gotten from some actors down in Austin, he directed the crowd and the cast.

At 10:00 A.M. the stands were empty.

By 11:00 they were half-full.

And by noon there was not a seat left for the 2:00 P.M. performance.

Nathan, Leah, Colin, and all the others gathered in the

barn by 12:30, with Miss D'Imperio giving last-minute coaching and finishing touches to the costumes.

Leah whispered, "Are you ready?"

"I think so. Are you?"

"Yeah . . . I guess. Nathan, would you pray for me?"

"Sure. I'm going to pray for all of us."

"No, I mean, would you pray just for me . . . right now?"

"Here?"

"Yeah?"

"Out loud?"

"Please!" Leah pleaded.

He cleared his throat and then began, "Ah . . . Lord, it's me, Nathan. We're all nervous here . . . and Leah, well she's really nervous. But we think we're doing the right thing—the right thing for Thunder, for the school, and for ourselves. But help us not to do anything that will make us ashamed. And 'specially help Leah remember her lines. Amen."

"Amen." She smiled, leaned over, and kissed Nathan on the cheek.

"What'd you do that for?" he demanded.

"It don't mean nothin'!" she insisted. "Thanks for praying."

Tension continued to build and reached its climax when Hawthorne H. Miller rushed into the barn at 1:53 P.M. shouting, "Line up, everyone! There's 1,212 paid customers waiting for a show!"

At exactly 2:00 P.M. the Galena Miners' Band began to play patriotic numbers. They ended with the "Star Spangled Banner" and Rena McGuire riding her palomino around the stockyard carrying the American flag. Just as the number concluded, her horse swung close to the pen where the bull, Lightning, was kept. He charged at the fence that separated them, making a terrible banging noise. Rena's startled horse reared up on his back legs, but she stood in the stirrups and waved the flag anyway—all of which brought thunderous applause from the audience.

Next came the wild horse riding. Six teams of three men each, including one team from the Running R, entered the arena on foot. They had to rope and saddle one of the six wild horses turned loose at the other end and ride one complete circle around the arena. The action was fast, turbulent, comical, scary, and skillful. The crowd loved it.

After that, Nathan, wearing a new bright blue shirt his mother had made for the occasion, raced out of the barn into the arena aboard Onepenny. He stood up on the saddle and trotted the spotted horse around the arena waving at the crowd. Then he sat down and worked the horse backwards, sideways, and through a number of spins. Finally, he raced Onepenny to the far end and brought him to a sliding stop. Then he called Leah out of the barn.

She walked out toward the middle of the arena just as they had practiced. Several men set out two barrels and placed a wooden plank across them. Right on cue, Leah's hat slipped off her head, but she continued to walk to the barrels. Nathan galloped across the dirt, leaned over, and scooped up her hat without even slowing down. The crowd roared its approval.

Then Leah climbed up on the plank and lay down, propping her head up on her elbow and smiling at the vast audience. Nathan swung Onepenny around one end of the arena and spurred him to a gallop, running straight at the reclining Leah. A gasp went up from the crowd as they sensed what was about to happen. Leah pinched her eyes shut. Nathan stood in the stirrups and leaned forward, and Onepenny leaped over the barrels, the plank, and Leah with plenty of room to spare.

At this, the crowd jumped to their feet and roared and applauded for several minutes, giving Nathan, Leah, and

Onepenny time to bow three times. Finally the three exited into the barn.

It took Hawthorne H. Miller screaming through his megaphone to get everyone's attention again for the dog act, the school Glee Club's medley of songs about mothers, and the Basque folk dancing. Then the trick-shot artist amazed them with his skills. His assistant tossed five glass balls into the air, and the man, riding horseback, blasted each one out of the sky before any hit the dirt.

When it was finally time for the play, Miss D'Imperio introduced the story of Esther, and the drama began. Everyone shouted out the lines on cue, and while Colin said all of his in a stilted monotone, no one missed a beat.

Not even when Leah caught her heel in her long dress and almost fell to the dirt.

Not even when Colin stopped in the middle of his lines and scratched his rash.

Not even when Nathan's costume tore as he bent low before the queen.

The day had been so hectic he hadn't even tried to remember his lines. They just seemed to roll out of his mouth. Before he knew it, he was calling out, "'And who knows whether you have come to the kingdom for such a time as this?'"

Leah, with hands folded over her heart, cried out, "'Go, gather together all the Jews in Shushan and fast for me, and neither eat nor drink for three days, night or day; my maidens and I will fast too, and then I will go to the king . . .'"

Nathan held his breath.

"'. . . which is not permitted by the law; and if I perish . . . I perish!'"

Applause and whistles rang through the bleachers, and Nathan winked at Leah. He had never seen her look so happy.

Thanks, Lord. Thanks a lot.

The play rolled to its conclusion with the hanging of the wicked Haman and the triumph of Mordecai, Queen Esther, and the Jews. In a burst of hometown pride, the people of Galena led the rest of the audience to stand to their feet and clap.

Back in the barn, Nathan pulled on his old clothes and brought Onepenny near the door. He could hear Hawthorne Miller on the megaphone building up the featured event.

"You riding back out?" Leah called up to him.

"Not unless Thunder needs help," he replied. "You did superior, Leah. Really grand!"

"Yeah. You did pretty good yourself."

"Well . . . this is it. We'll see what Thunder can do."

"What do you think will happen?"

"I have no idea, Leah—no idea at all."

According to a prearranged plan, Nathan's dad opened the gate and let the buffalo into the arena first. He started to trot across the huge corral, but suddenly he glanced up at the cheering crowd. He sat down on his haunches. His rear end was on the dirt, but his front feet held his massive head high.

Then the cowboys from the Running R let the fighting bull run into the arena. Instantly sensing the buffalo's presence, the bull pawed, snorted, and circled the arena once on a trot. The second time around he looked at Thunder eye to eye and suddenly spun and dashed full steam right at the buffalo.

"Get up, Thunder!" Nathan screamed from the barn door where he and Leah were watching. "Stand up! Don't let him hit you sitting down!"

The collision of the two skulls sounded like a rifle shot. The bull bounced back about six feet, and Thunder remained passive on his rear. The entire audience of 1,212 rose to their feet, screaming at the top of their lungs.

Reeling back to the rail, the bull circled the buffalo once more. This time he trotted several laps around the rim of the arena before turning and making a ferocious dash toward the buffalo.

Thunder stood to his feet and lowered his head. The audience gritted their teeth in anticipation of the horrible crunch. Once again it sounded more like an explosion than a collision.

The bull bounced back fifteen feet, staggered to keep its balance, and retreated to the rail. Thunder, now up on all fours, stood immobile in the middle of the arena. With the crowd's roar at a near-deafening level, the bull circled the arena several more times. He stopped to glance at Thunder several times and then continued his circling.

For a while Nathan thought maybe the contest was over. He kept looking at the Running R cowboys, but they were busy yelling insults at their bull.

Finally, coming around to the buffalo's back side, the bull pawed the dirt, snorted, and once again charged. This time Thunder spun on his hoofs and ran headlong into the charging bull.

The shattering crash silenced the crowd completely. The bull, thrown some twenty feet away, pitched and wobbled, fell to its knees, struggled back to his feet, and then staggered toward the fence. Again the animal circled the arena, not looking at the buffalo, but only at the fence.

"What's he doing?" Leah called.

"Looking for a gate to get out." Nathan smiled.

Finally, the bull cut across the arena on a dead run away from the stands full of people, leaped the back fence, taking the top rail with him, and headed out into the sage-covered prairie east of Galena.

Thunder stood still as the crowd tossed their hats, fired

guns into the air, and shouted. Nathan noticed the buffalo's left eye blink twice and then stay shut.

"What's Thunder doing?" Leah shouted.

"I think he's taking a nap!" Nathan laughed. "We're going to Carson City! We're really going!"

He grabbed Leah by the waist, and they danced around the barn.

9

On May 4 at 9:00 A.M., "Mercee's Buffalo-Tight #1" rolled out of Galena, Nevada. In the four-wheeled iron pen was a 2,500-pound buffalo. Leah Walker and Miss D'Imperio rode next to Mr. Mercee, and Nathan Riggins and Colin Maddison, Jr., (with two *d*'s) rode their horses alongside the wagon.

Tona was locked in the woodshed behind the Riggins house, scheduled to be released the next day. The plan was to take six days to travel to Carson City. Then there would be a ceremony with the governor and a guided tour of the capital. Miss D'Imperio, the children, and the two horses would return on the train (a trip donated by Mr. Pennington) to Battle Mountain Station. Mr. Mercee would either sell the wagon in Carson City or drive it back to Galena.

The first evening they camped in Star City, where they were welcomed at the school like conquering heroes. In Lovelock the next night, they formed a parade down Main Street, with the iron wagon and buffalo winding up at the county courthouse. The third night out, they slept on the ground south of the train tracks at Hobner's Well—the last drinking water before crossing the eastern part of the Carson Sink on the way to Ragtown. They laughed, giggled, and talked into the night until Miss D'Imperio finally announced it was time for bed.

They fastened the horses and mules to a picket line, and Thunder sprawled on the straw with his legs tucked under him in the iron wagon. Miss D'Imperio and Leah used a small tent. Nathan, Colin, and Abel Mercee slept next to the wagon. Originally they considered sleeping under the wagon, but neither boy liked the idea of a 2,500 pound buffalo perched above them.

It was well after dark when a stiff breeze from the west began to blow. The temperature began to drop, and Nathan could see clouds rolling across the star-covered sky. Mr. Mercee stood barefoot on his bedroll studying the clouds.

Nathan crawled out and pulled on his boots.

"Is that a storm rolling in?"

"Yep."

"Will it rain?"

"Could be. We can't take a chance. We better move out."

"In the dark?"

"It's better than sitting here. Wake Colin. I'll signal the women."

With the whole crew dressed and partly awake, Mr. Mercee addressed them. "If it rains, this sink will fill up, and we'll find ourselves in a lake instead of a dry lake bed. If the ground between here and Ragtown gets wet at all, this wagon will bog past its axles, and I doubt if anything short of a locomotive could pull it out."

"What are you suggesting?" Miss D'Imperio asked.

"We need to make a run for Ragtown tonight. The closer we get, the closer we'll be to someone who can help us if we do get stuck. So load up all the drinking water you can. I'll hitch the team."

"How can we see where to go?" Leah asked.

"Nathan and that spotted horse can lead the way. I'll

need Mr. Maddison, Jr., here to ride the lead mule and call back Nathan's directions."

With a cooling wind and a sense of urgency, they packed up quickly and began the trek across the lake bed. Nathan had brought only a light ducking jacket, and he now had it buttoned at the neck and the collar turned up. His hat was screwed down and held in place by a horsehair stampede string. He leaned over Onepenny's neck and kept peering into the blackness of the night, searching for any faint sign of previous wagon tracks.

He shouted directions, which were echoed in the wind by Colin and repeated with a shout by Abel Mercee. Leah and Miss D'Imperio huddled under a blanket and tried to doze off amid the shouts. Only Thunder relaxed. He slept peacefully as long as the wagon rolled.

Sometime in the middle of the night—somewhere in the middle of the Carson Sink—it began to rain. It was just a few drops . . . just a sprinkle . . . then a little more . . . then a little more.

"Head us toward any high ground you can find!" Mercee shouted.

"Head toward high ground!" Colin repeated.

"Toward high ground!" Nathan answered.

The wagon began to sink a bit into the mud, and the mules struggled to pull it. In the brief seconds when lightning lit the sky, Nathan thought he spied some low-lying hills to the south. He signaled the wagon toward them. He wasn't at all sure how far away they might be.

The rain slapped his face now, and the mules were taking one labored step at a time. The wagon wheels left foot-deep slimy ruts. Nathan suddenly felt an incline under Onepenny's feet. He climbed up what turned out to be no more than a mound. But it was a mound big enough for a wagon and several horses.

Now soaked to the bone, he rode back and grabbed the lead mule's halter, helping to pull its head up the hill. When the wagon crested, he stopped the team and rode back to Mr. Mercee.

Shouting through the rain, he explained the situation. "If this lake bed gets some water in it, we're better off up here!"

"You're right," Mercee shouted. "We'll stop here! Set up the women's tent. I'll tend to the mules."

"Tent?"

"At least it will get the wind off them!"

"Yes, sir!"

Sloshing in the mud, Nathan put up the little tent, and the drenched women stumbled inside. Both of them had dry clothes in a valise they had brought, but they huddled close, trying to overcome the cold.

Mercee, Riggins, and Maddison threw a tarp down in the mud and crawled under the right side of the wagon. None of them mentioned the buffalo above them.

"I don't see why we can't all get into that tent!" Colin whimpered.

"It ain't proper!" Mercee bellowed. "I've got firewood slung under here, but it wouldn't burn in a downpour like this! We'll have to wait it out."

All three pulled wet blankets around their soaked shoulders and tried to think of dryer days.

A good hour before the sun came up, the rain stopped, and a warm southern breeze began to blow. Immediately, Abel Mercee pulled out the wood and built a fire. Within minutes around the blaze, Nathan felt warmness return to his fingers and face. The women stayed inside the tent while the men changed into their driest clothing. Then everyone gathered around the fire to dry out their wet things.

"What are we going to find at daylight?" Nathan asked Mr. Mercee.

"Well, we'll either be on an island in a lake, or the lake bed will soak all the water in, and there'll be powder on top."

"Powder?" Colin asked.

"Alkali! It leeches right up out of the ground and dries the moisture. But it can be tricky—dusty on top and sticky gumbo one inch below."

"How close are we to Ragtown?" Miss D'Imperio asked.

"I'm not sure. Maybe morning will tell."

■

It didn't.

The sun came up. The warm southern wind continued to blow, but they could see only alkali in every direction.

No trees.

No sage.

No grass.

No roads.

No houses.

No chocolate creme fills.

Nothing.

After a big breakfast of boiled eggs, sausage, and beans, they all stood by the fire and stared south.

"It's crusted up, Nathan," Mr. Mercee noted. "I believe a horse might walk out there."

"You want me to try it?"

"Yeah, ride south to those next hills, climb them, and take a look. Come back and tell me what you see."

Dry powder covered the barren, white ground that a few

hours earlier had been slick with a slimy mud. The crust held under Onepenny's hoofs. Wind blew the white dirt all around, and soon Nathan's lips were chapped and his eyes burned.

He reached the hills in less than an hour and from the top could only see more alkali . . . and on the distant horizon what looked like trees.

"If there are trees, there has to be water! Good water!" he shouted at his spotted horse. Staring back the way he had come, he could barely make out the wagon. He tried to determine a straight line between the trees to the south and the wagon to the north. Then he piled dry alkali chucks on top of each other for a marker.

Turning to ride back, he thought he saw a dust devil blowing near the wagon. Then he realized that it was riders coming up from the south.

"They can help us pull that iron wagon over to the trees! But where in the world did they come from?"

He wanted to gallop up and join in the greetings, but he knew that the crust would only hold Onepenny at a fast walk. Coming within sight, he noticed two new horses tied behind the iron wagon and a stranger working with the harness of the lead mule. No one else was in sight. The man tipped his hat as Nathan rode up.

"Howdy!"

"Where is everyone?" Nathan demanded.

"Now which everyone did you mean?" The man grinned.

"Mr. Mercee, Leah, Colin, Miss D'Imperio!" he called, slowly reaching over to unbutton his rifle scabbard.

"Leave it, boy!" a voice shouted from behind the wagon. Suddenly, a man wearing woolly chaps stepped out holding a short shotgun on Leah and Miss D'Imperio.

"Climb off that spotted horse!" he demanded.

"Mourning and Early?" Nathan mumbled.

"Well, isn't that nice. The boy knows our names."

"Leah, Miss D., are you all right?"

"Be careful, Nathan. These men are dangerous," Miss D'Imperio warned.

"Oowhee, listen to the schoolteacher. We are armed and dangerous, boy."

Nathan climbed off Onepenny and stepped toward Leah.

"Where's Mr. Mercee and Colin?" he asked.

"The blacksmith bumped his head on the end of my shotgun, so he's napping it out under the wagon," one of the men said.

"And Mr. Pink Cheeks is up there with the buffalo!"

"Pink Cheeks?"

"They put Colin in with Thunder," Leah explained.

Nathan stared into the cage and saw a tied, gagged, and frightened Colin standing next to a hay-chewing buffalo.

"Colin identified them as soon as they rode up, and there was a scuffle. Mr. Mercee took several blows to the head," Miss D'Imperio informed him.

"Now there is no need to worry, boy. We'll leave you and your friend up there with the buffalo. We'll just take the horses, mules, belongings, water, and womenfolk. You can have all the rest." They laughed.

"The women?" Nathan shouted.

"Why, we want to make sure they're good and safe —right, Early?"

"That's right. I sure do like that horse, boy. I think I'll have him for my own."

"You can't—," Nathan started to yell and then found himself looking down the barrel of a drawn and cocked .45. He stood in place while the gunman mounted Onepenny.

"Stay, Onepenny, stay!" Nathan yelled.

The man kicked his spurs into the spotted horse's flanks, but Onepenny didn't move.

"Nathan, I don't know what to do!" Miss D'Imperio moaned with a high, tight voice.

"Stay, Onepenny!"

The outlaw kicked the horse again, and this time the horse began to buck.

"Nathan," Leah yelled, "'who knows whether you have come to the kingdom for such a time as this?'"

She's right, Lord! I couldn't live with myself if I didn't try something!

He finished, "'And if I perish . . . I perish.'"

On the third buck the outlaw flew off Onepenny's back. Before he could get to his feet, Nathan jumped into the saddle and spurred Onepenny out into the alkali flats. To Nathan's surprise the ground held up fine.

"I'll shoot him!" one of the outlaws shouted.

"Don't hit that horse! I still want that horse!" the other demanded.

One of the men ran to the back of the wagon and began to mount his horse to pursue. Nathan plowed toward the other outlaw. By dropping to the right side of the horse, Indian-style, Nathan made it impossible for the man to shoot him. In the confusion both women broke free and began to run out into the Sink.

Gaining on the confused gunman, Nathan leaned way forward in the stirrups and gave Onepenny the command to jump.

He's never jumped over a man before. I don't think he can do it. I hope he can't do it!

Onepenny's flying legs caught the man in the chest, knocking him violently to the ground. The man didn't move.

Nathan spun toward the other man, who fired a wild

shot and climbed onto his horse. Pulling his rifle out of the scabbard, Nathan raced after him. But the man's horse hit a bog only a few feet from the wagon.

The horse came to a complete stop.

The outlaw didn't.

He flew headlong into the alkali dust.

Nathan sprang down off Onepenny and jammed the barrel of the rifle against the back of the man's head.

"This thing is cocked, Mister, and I'm mighty nervous. If you so much as wiggle, the hair trigger is going to go off, and I won't be able to stop it! Leah!" he shouted. "Bring me a rope."

Within minutes Nathan had both men tied, hands and feet. Miss D'Imperio helped Mr. Mercee sit up next to the wagon. He had several red welts on his face and head. As Nathan walked over to them, Leah ran up and hugged Onepenny. "Old Onepenny really came through, didn't he?" She smiled.

"Onepenny? How about me?"

Speaking under her breath, Leah replied, "I can't hug you in front of Miss D'Imperio. It wouldn't be proper!"

Nathan nodded and went over to the others. Miss D'Imperio jumped up and gave Nathan a big hug. He winked at Leah when he caught her eye.

"Nathan," Miss D'Imperio said, "it might seem foolish later on—whenever I think about it—but that was about the bravest thing I've ever seen. I've never needed to be rescued before, and I hope I never will again, but I thank the Lord that you and your spotted horse were with us!"

"I just had to try something. Those lines me and Leah said . . . well, we weren't play-acting today."

Then a frantic protest came from the iron cage. Nathan crawled up and pulled Colin out. Finally, untied and ungagged,

Colin shouted, "Kill them! They deserve to be shot and left out in this barren land!"

"Don't mind him." Nathan grinned. "It's Colin's reaction to every personal injustice."

■

It was noon before Mr. Mercee pronounced the dirt dry enough to hold the weight of the wagon. When they pulled out this time, all took their original places, except that Thunder now had two passengers in the cage with him and two horses trailed behind the wagon.

After refilling with fresh water and washing their faces at the spring near the clump of trees Nathan had spotted early that morning, they continued south. About sunset a group of concerned citizens from Ragtown rode out and found them. A big party was planned for that night, and the hosts had been worried about the travelers.

■

With Mourning and Early in the Churchill County Jail, and after a bath and a change of clothes, they all went to the party.

Miss D'Imperio visited with a long line of young men.

Mr. Mercee talked wagons with several local merchants.

Leah wouldn't let go of Nathan's arm.

And Colin hovered over plates full of cookies.

10

*T*he state of Nevada, searching for an excuse to celebrate, found it in the "Last Buffalo Capital Expedition," as it was now being called in the newspapers. The capture of Early and Mourning—two otherwise petty thieving misfits from upstate New York—was described as a heroic battle for Nevada's cultural heritage.

When "Mercee's Buffalo-Tight #1" swayed out of Ragtown, they had twenty-six well-armed outriders as escort. By the time they reached Gold Hill, the party had swelled to over a hundred. After a parade through every dusty street of Gold Hill, the mayor of Virginia City insisted that they come on up the mountain to the "Queen City of the Comstock."

A series of hurried telegraphs to Governor Kinkead postponed the Carson City festivities one day and allowed them a trip to Virginia City. By the time they creaked their way into the famous mining town, Fourth of July bunting draped the buildings. Miners, gamblers, shop clerks, and families crammed the wooden sidewalks.

Nathan waited aboard Onepenny for the Virginia City Marching Band to line up and lead the procession. He rode up to the wagon and looked at Leah and Miss D'Imperio.

"I don't get it. This is really not such a big deal, is it, Miss D'Imperio? I mean, a buffalo is a buffalo."

Miss D'Imperio opened her salmon-colored parasol to

shade her eyes. "Nathan, Nevada's a tough state—hardworking men and women. Everyone's trying to make some money, and most plan to leave as soon as they make their fortune. Not much future for a state like that."

She pulled off her white gloves and held them in her lap. "But you and Leah and Colin—you represent the future of Nevada. You might be the first children to do something, anything for the betterment this state. Your determination to get the buffalo to Carson City is telling folks, 'Hey, this is our state too!' I think it's made people believe Nevada is more than just a mining camp. You've inspired some folks to think beyond the daily grind. You gave them a breath of fresh air, and in a mining state there isn't much fresh air."

That evening at a picnic, the Galena group sat at honored places. Miss D'Imperio presented a short talk on how the whole school had worked on the project. And Mr. Mercee was allowed to make a pitch for his buffalo-tight wagons.

Right after a big breakfast the next morning, they started out toward Carson City. Most estimates placed the number of people traveling with them in excess of five hundred.

Under Mr. Pennington's planning and leadership, Carson City was ready for the Last Buffalo Capital Expedition. A stout iron corral had been constructed a block south of the capital building. A large, freshly painted sign marked the location. It gave special thanks to the "Galena School, Lander County, and their teacher Miss Angelica D'Imperio."

When Leah read the sign, she turned to Nathan and whispered, "I didn't know her name was Angelica! Did you?"

"Nope," Nathan replied. "But it fits, doesn't it?"

They unloaded Thunder, and he trotted around the entire corral, occasionally testing the strength of the iron posts with a head butt.

The parade in Carson City was the largest and most

orderly of the trip. Mr. Pennington decided to spread out the Galena group in order to lengthen the procession.

First came Nathan on Onepenny, then Colin, now sporting his famous woolly chaps. Then, in a special coach donated for the occasion by the Sierra Vista Carriage Works, Leah Walker would roll along wearing a bright yellow dress given to her by Marquette Millinery. Following Leah, in an open coach that had been used at the governor's inauguration, came Miss D'Imperio, wearing another Marquette creation of off-white and lavender.

Finally, with an escort of fifty musket-carrying men dressed in buckskins from the Ormsby County Mountain Men Association, would come Mr. Abel Mercee, his all-iron wagon, and Thunder—"the last buffalo in Nevada."

At the final minute Nathan was handed an American flag to carry. He decided to stand in the saddle as he rode down the street waving the flag. But then he had second thoughts.

Lord, this is all . . . you know, kind of out of hand, isn't it? Help me to enjoy the fun of it all, but not take it too serious. It's sort of a good day to be me . . . and Leah and Colin and Miss D'Imperio and Mr. Mercee . . . and even Thunder. Thanks, Lord, from all of us.

The parade was late in starting. Something created a disturbance in the rear. Nathan rode back to Colin.

"What's happening back there?"

Colin shrugged, "I don't know . . . maybe Mr. Mercee's having trouble with the wagon. Say, Nathan, do you really think I should wear the woollies? I mean, it's a might warm on a day like this. Yet they are rather glorious-looking, don't you think?"

"Eh . . . sure. Definitely wear them. I'm going to check this out."

"But you'll need to hold your place," Colin insisted.

121

"You hold it for me," Nathan called. He trotted up the parade route. "Leah, you look . . ." His voice faded.

"I look what?" She squinted her eyes and wrinkled her nose.

"You look about sixteen years old and extremely pretty," he blurted out and hurried past her. Miss D'Imperio was visiting with a tall, strong-looking man on a beautiful black horse, so Nathan just tipped his hat and rode on.

Once he made it past the Mountain Man club, he found Mr. Mercee and several men on horseback trying to get Thunder out of his corral and into the wagon.

"Nathan!" Mercee shouted. "We can't get him to move. Perhaps you could help!"

"I can't blame him. Six days in that jail cell, and he has no intention of returning. Maybe we should just leave him corralled."

"My heavens, no!" exclaimed Mr. Pennington. "The whole town is waiting to see Thunder roll down Carson Street."

Nathan handed the American flag over to Mr. Mercee and rode Onepenny into the iron corral. Thunder, who had absolutely refused to budge for all the others, glanced up at the spotted pony. Nathan ran Onepenny right at the big buffalo and then, as usual, veered off to the right. True to form, Thunder waved his head at the horse and began to trot after him.

Nathan circled the corral twice with the buffalo trailing behind. Several days cooped up in the wagon had stiffened the old buffalo, and Nathan could see him slowing down, yet trying to chase the spotted horse. As he rounded the open gate, Nathan grabbed the American flag and shouted at Mr. Pennington, "Get the parade started! Thunder isn't going back into that wagon!"

Parade participants parted as Onepenny with a flag-waving Nathan proceeded up Carson Street, Thunder trotting behind. While the rest of the parade struggled to catch up, the crowds lining the streets cheered in wild enthusiasm.

Thunder, bewildered by all the confusion, followed the only familiar sight—the spotted horse—straight up Carson Street, around the corner on East William, and back down Stewart to the corral.

He and Nathan finished the parade route well ahead of the others, but no one seemed to mind. With Thunder happy to be back with his hay and a bucket of sweet oats, Nathan led Onepenny out of the corral and then closed and locked the big iron gate.

Everyone was either still in the parade or watching it, so Nathan slid down off his horse, loosed his cinch, and led the spotted horse to the water trough.

"Well, Onepenny, we did it, didn't we? I think I'm going to miss that buffalo. He looks sort of lonesome. You're about the only friend he has!"

"Hey, cowboy, do you always talk to your horse?"

Pushing his hat back, he looked up to see a girl riding a tall black horse.

"Tashawna?"

"Hi, Nathan."

"What are you doing h-here?" he stammered.

"I live here, remember?"

"Oh, yeah, I guess I forgot."

"Out of sight, out of mind." She smiled.

"What?"

"Oh . . . nothing. Listen, this was a great parade. I couldn't believe it was really you when I read it in the paper. You're a hero!"

"Yeah. It's all kind of silly, isn't it?" he admitted.

"Enjoy it, I say. There'll be enough bad days that will come along. That's what my daddy always says."

"Your dad! The black horse! Your father's in Carson City now?"

"Yeah. He came here about two weeks after me and Mom. Of course he doesn't live with us."

"He doesn't? Where does he live?"

"Down there in that granite building."

"The Nevada State Prison?"

"Yeah . . . but only until next December."

"So he turned himself in for that stage robbery?"

"Yep. He said it was the proper thing to do."

"Well . . . how . . . how are you and your mom getting along?"

"Mama's working for a doctor, and I'm taking care of some horses for Mr. and Mrs. Pennington. We'll get by."

"That's great, Tashawna!"

She climbed down off her horse and tied him to a rail. Then she and Nathan walked over to the corral and peered through at Thunder.

"You know what I kept thinking about when I saw all of you riding in the parade?" she asked.

"What?"

"Well, if we'd have listened to your advice and stayed in Galena, maybe I'd be right out there with you."

"Yeah." Nathan nodded. "I'm sure you would have. You could even have done some trick riding or something!"

"Hey, I'm taking some singing lessons. Isn't that something?"

"You told me you'd be singing at the opera house some day."

"Yep. Miss Tashawna Cholach—on stage!" She giggled.

"You've got to save me some tickets, remember?"

"I promise."

Nathan noticed that others from the parade were starting to pull up to the iron corral behind them.

"You know, Nathan, someday . . . someday I'm going to be in a grand parade too. I won't be just a country girl from some remote ranch. I won't be some stage robber's daughter. I'll be famous!"

"Tashawna, I sure hope your dreams all come true . . . and they don't disappoint you when they do. Listen, when you ride in that parade, be sure and look in the crowd 'cause I'll be there cheering you on."

"Who knows? Maybe Nathan T. Riggins of Lander County will be riding with me. Maybe he'll be governor by then."

"I doubt that," Nathan mumbled.

"Nathan, can I ride Onepenny—just for old time's sake?"

He took off his hat and swept it low in front of Tashawna. "Miss, I'd be delighted to have you ride my talented pony!"

"Uhhum!"

Nathan turned around to see Leah, carrying a yellow parasol, standing behind them.

"Oh! Hi!," he called. "Wasn't the parade spectacular?"

"Up to this point," Leah huffed, tugging to make her dress feel more comfortable.

"Oh . . ." He turned to Tashawna. "You remember—"

"Your dear little friend from Galena!" Tashawna smirked.

"This is," Nathan's voice sounded deep and deliberate, "my girlfriend Leah."

A burst of joy swept across Leah's face, lighting her eyes and lifting her smile. She stepped up to Nathan and slipped her arm in his.

"Nathan, darlin', the governor is expecting us for a cook-out at his house. Perhaps your friend, Miss Curlylocks, wouldn't mind putting Onepenny in the stable when she's through with her ride."

She tugged Nathan over toward the smiling governor, Mr. Pennington, and the others.

Leah glanced back at Tashawna.

Nathan didn't.

If he had, he would have seen both girls sticking their tongues out.